Brandon reached for her hand and pointed toward the water.

They sat in silence, watching as the sun set in a blaze of orange and reds across the sky. "It's amazing." And so was he. How many men would be content to sit and enjoy the simple pleasure of a sunset?

"I agree." Their eyes met. "Stunning."

The intensity of his stare told her he meant more than the sunset. She gently withdrew her hand and resumed eating.

When they finished, he settled the bill and asked, "Would you like to take a walk?"

"I'd love to." Because they were close to the water, the temperatures had dipped and a slight breeze had kicked up.

He entwined their fingers and they strolled off. He stopped a ways down the path and faced her. For a moment, he said nothing, seemingly struggling with what he wanted to say.

"What is it?"

"I can show you better than I can tell you," Brandon whispered and lowered his head.

Dear Reader,

I hope you have enjoyed reading about the Gray siblings as much as I have writing them! Many of you have asked when will Brandon Gray's story be told and here he is. You know how intense he is and how often he sticks his foot in his mouth. Well…nothing has changed, lol. Only this time he's met his match in a woman who might just make him want to readjust a bit. Faith Alexander has no qualms about sending Brandon packing, and I totally delighted in watching the sparks fly…in more ways than one. And I hope you enjoy the ride, as well.

Up next is Khalil Gray—model turned fitness buff, and boy, do I have a lot in store for him! Stay tuned.

As always, I so appreciate all your love and support. Without you, I couldn't do this.

Much love,

Sheryl

Website: SherylLister.com

Email: sheryllister@gmail.com

Facebook: Facebook.com/SherylListerAuthor

Twitter: Twitter.com/1Slynne

Giving My all to You

SHERYL LISTER

HARLEQUIN® KIMANI™ ROMANCE

Recycling programs
for this product may
not exist in your area.

ISBN-13: 978-0-373-86498-0

Giving My All to You

Copyright © 2017 by Sheryl Lister

HARLEQUIN®

Printed in U.S.A.

™ www.Harlequin.com

Sheryl Lister has enjoyed reading and writing for as long as she can remember. She writes contemporary and inspirational romance and romantic suspense. She's been nominated for an Emma Award and an RT Reviewers' Choice Best Book Award and has been named BRAB's 2015 Best New Author. When she's not reading, writing or playing chauffeur, Sheryl can be found on a date with her husband or in the kitchen creating appetizers and bite-size desserts. Sheryl resides in California and is a wife, mother of three daughters and a son-in-love, and grandmother to two very special little boys.

Books by Sheryl Lister

Harlequin Kimani Romance

Just to Be with You
All of Me
It's Only You
Tender Kisses
Places in My Heart
Unwrapping the Holidays with Nana Malone
Giving My All to You

Visit the Author Profile page
at Harlequin.com for more titles.

For the readers who asked for Brandon's story.

Acknowledgments
My Heavenly Father, thank You for my life.
You never cease to amaze me with Your blessings!

To my husband, Lance, my children,
family and friends. Thank you for your continued support.
I appreciate and love you!

To my critique partner, Leslie Wright. Girl,
those phone calls are a lifesaver! Thanks, sis.

A special thank-you to the readers and authors I've met
on this journey. You continue to enrich my life.

Thank you to my editor, Patience Bloom,
for your editorial guidance and support.

A very special thank-you to my agent, Sarah E. Younger.
I appreciate you more than words can say.

Chapter 1

"Hey, girl. You want to do lunch today?"

Faith Alexander smiled. "Sure. I'm just working on one of my web designs." Once or twice a month on a Saturday she and her best friend, Kathi Norris, met for lunch. "Hang on, Kathi. Someone's at the door," she said. She saved the page she'd been working on and left the spare bedroom in her town house that she had converted to an office. It contained a desk, two bookshelves, a file cabinet and a sofa for those times when she planned to work all night, but needed a place to nap. She crossed the living room, opened the door and saw the mailman standing there.

He stuck a box into her hands along with a card and pen. "Just sign here, please."

She cradled the phone against her ear, adjusted the box and signed the receipt. "Thank you." Faith closed the door and frowned, not recognizing the sender.

"Helloooo."

Kathi's voice drew Faith out of her thoughts. "Sorry. I

just got a box from someone in Los Angeles named Thaddeus Whitcomb."

"Ooh, girl, you've got a man sending you gifts from California?"

"No. I have no idea who this is." She shook the box and heard a slight rustling.

"What's in it?"

"I have no idea," she said, walking back to her office and placing it on the desk.

"Anyway, Cameron—the guy I've been dating—has a cute friend and I thought we could double-date," Kathi said.

"No."

"Come on, Faith."

"*No*. The last time I went on one of your little blind double dates it turned into the month from hell. You're on your own this time."

"Grant wasn't that bad."

"Hmph. You weren't the one he was calling ten times a day asking when I was going to let him come to my house. I swear that man had octopus arms and was just as slimy. He made my skin crawl." She shivered with the remembrance.

"Okay, okay, I get your point. He did border on stalking."

"You think?"

"But this guy is different—six feet, rich brown skin, fit and easy on the eyes."

"Doesn't matter. I'm not interested." After that fiasco six months ago, she had sworn off men and was content with building her year-old web design business.

"We aren't getting any younger and I'd like to settle down and have a kid or two before my eggs shrivel up and die."

She laughed. "Kathi, you act like we're pushing fifty.

We're only thirty." She cut into the box, pulled back the flap and saw a stack of letters with a rubber band around them. All were addressed to her from Thaddeus Whitcomb and had "Return to Sender" written on them. She quickly flipped through them and noted the postmarks went back almost twenty-eight years.

While half listening to Kathi list all the reasons why this guy would be different, Faith opened the gray envelope on the top that had her first name written in large letters and withdrew the sheet of paper. When she unfolded it, a photo of a man wearing an army uniform and holding a baby fell out. She didn't know who he was, but she recognized the child. She quickly read the letter. Her eyes widened and her heart stopped and started up again. "It can't be. He's supposed to be dead," she whispered in shock. "Kathi, I have to go."

"Wait…what? What about lunch?"

"I need to take a rain check. I'll call you later."

Butterflies fluttered in her belly as she picked up the photo again and studied it for a moment before rereading the letter. Tears filled her eyes and anger rose within her. She tossed everything back into the box, slid her arms into a light jacket and grabbed the box, her purse and keys, and left. Although the sun shone, there was a slight breeze and the early June temperatures in Portland hovered near seventy. Twenty minutes later, she rang her parents' doorbell.

"Faith," her father said with a wide grin, "we didn't know you were coming over. Come in, baby." He kissed her cheek.

"Hi, Dad." Her mother had married William Alexander when Faith was eight and he had been the only father she'd known. "Where's Mom?"

"She's in the family room working on one of those word search puzzles." He placed a hand on her arm as she passed him. "Everything okay, Faith?"

"I don't think so."

His concerned gazed roamed over her face. "Well, let's go talk about it."

Her mother glanced up from her book when they entered and lowered the recliner. "Hey, sweetheart."

"We need to talk, Mom."

Her mother's brows knit together. "Something wrong?"

Faith dropped the box on her mother's lap.

"What is this?"

"You tell me."

Her mother lifted out the envelopes and quickly flipped through them. Her loud gasp pierced the silence. "Where... where did you get these?"

"They were delivered to my house this afternoon. How could you do this to me, Mom?" She paced back and forth across the plush gray carpet.

"What the heck is going on here?" her father asked. "Who are those letters from?"

She stopped pacing and, not taking her eyes off her mother, Faith answered, "My father. The man she told me died while serving in the army."

His eyes widened and he dragged a hand down his face. "Francis? Is that true?" he asked.

Her mother tossed the letters aside. "You don't understand," she snapped.

"You're right, I don't." Faith flopped down onto the sofa. "He's been alive all this time and trying to contact me," she murmured, tears gathering in her eyes. "Why, Mom? Why did you lie to me?"

"I was trying to protect you."

"*Protect me?* From what?"

"You were too young to know what it was like when he came home that last time—the crying out, the nightmares with him flailing around the bed, the flashbacks. I was worried he'd hurt you and me, and I didn't want to deal with it every time he came home." She sniffed. "So I left."

Faith couldn't begin to imagine what her father had seen and experienced that would cause such nightmares, but she had a hard time believing that her mom hadn't even tried to help him. Growing up, she'd always marveled at her mother's compassionate nature and wanted to grow up to be just like her. Now she was learning that hadn't always been the case. "That still didn't give you the right to just erase him from my life." Faith wiped away her own tears. "And how did you know you would have to deal with it every time?" She paused. "He's invited me to visit him and I'm going."

Her mother jumped up from the chair. "Why? It's been twenty-eight years. What can you possibly gain by going to see him? Just let it be."

"He's my *father* and I'm not going to let it be." She caught her stepfather's gaze. "I'm sorry, Dad. You know I love you." She felt bad because he had always been there for her.

He nodded. "I know, honey. You go do what you have to do. Francis, she has to find her own way."

"Thanks, Dad."

The two women engaged in a staredown for a full minute before her mother turned away. She had never been this angry with her mother. Sure, when Faith was a teen, they'd had their disagreements, but nothing like this.

Her mother pointed a finger Faith's way. "Nothing good can come from this. *Nothing.* I don't know why he's trying to disrupt your life after all these years."

Faith threw up her hands. "Disrupt my life? How is wanting to know your daughter a disruption?" She snatched up the letters. "He's been sending letters for twenty-eight years and you sent them back without ever telling me. The only person who's *disrupted* my life is you." She put the letters in the box and stormed past her mother. "I have to get out of here."

At the door, her stepfather's voice stopped her.

"I know you're pretty angry at your mother right now, but try to see it from her side. She was only doing what she thought best." He gave her a strong hug, palmed her face much like he did when she was a child and placed a gentle kiss on her forehead. "Whatever you decide, I'll always be here." Although approaching his fifty-eighth birthday, he didn't look a day over forty. His walnut-colored skin remained unlined, his body was still trim and toned, and his deep brown eyes held the love he had always shown her.

"Thanks, Dad."

"When are you leaving?"

"I don't know."

"Call to let us know you're safe."

"I will." Faith kissed his cheek and slipped out the door.

She drove home still in disbelief over what her mother had done and that her biological father was actually alive. Once there, she called Kathi and filled her in, then searched hotels and reserved a flight and car for the following Tuesday. Although she loved her stepfather, Faith had often imagined what kind of man her father had been. Now that she had his letters, she'd get her wish. But she wanted to know what he would be like in person. *Guess I'll find out soon.*

"Are you ready to step into the CEO position, little brother?"

Brandon Gray acknowledged a couple of people leaving the conference room after the Wednesday morning staff meeting ended. He then smiled at his older sister, Siobhan. "Been ready." His father had started the company more than two decades ago after being discharged from the army. When he saw the difficulties his best friend, who had been wounded in combat, had trying to get services and accommodations, Nolan Gray decided, instead of waiting around, he would design them himself. What started in their home garage had now grown to be one of the largest in-home safety companies in the country. They provided everything from shower rails and specialized mattresses to custom-built ramps. Their father would step down at the end of the month, leaving Brandon as head of Gray Home Safety. His father's best friend, Thaddeus Whitcomb, whom they affectionately called Uncle Thad, had joined the company shortly after it was formed and served as the company's vice president. He planned to retire, as well. The two men had always said that the reins would be turned over to their children, with a Gray in the CEO position and a Whitcomb as vice president.

Siobhan stuffed some papers into a folder. "I wonder what Uncle Thad is going to do. Too bad he never got married or had kids. And as good-looking as he is, I'm surprised. I don't ever remember seeing him date."

"I saw one woman coming around for a while when I was working in the warehouse that summer after junior year in high school, but I don't know what happened to her."

"Well, with no one to step in as vice president, you'll be in charge of everything."

"True." Brandon actually preferred it that way, expected it after all this time. While the roles worked well for his dad and uncle, he'd much rather work solo.

Their father came around the table. "Brandon, can you come by my office? I need to talk to you."

Brandon studied his father's serious expression. "Sure, Dad. I'll be right there."

His father clapped him on the shoulder and exited.

Siobhan said, "I wonder what that's about."

He shrugged. "I don't know."

"Well, let me know what happens."

"Okay." Brandon left the room and started down the corridor leading to his father's office. He spoke to the administrative assistant, who told him to go in.

"I just hope this time you can get the answers," he heard his father say.

"Dad? Oh, hey, Unc. I didn't know you were here."

"Hi, Brandon. I'll talk to you later, Nolan," Uncle Thad said. The two older men shared a glance that wasn't lost on Brandon.

He followed his uncle's departure. Today Uncle Thad was on crutches. He'd lost the lower part of his left leg during Desert Storm and typically used a prosthetic. However, over the past year, he had taken to using his wheelchair or the crutches because of problems with the artificial limb.

After Uncle Thad left, Brandon's father said, "Close the door and have a seat, son."

He complied. "What's going on, Dad?"

"There may be a little delay in you taking my position."

"What? Why?"

"Something has come up that needs to be handled before we pass on the reins."

"If you tell me what it is, maybe I can help."

"No, no," his father answered quickly. "I'll handle it."

He tried to keep his surprise and distress hidden. Brandon knew he could be intense sometimes, but he was the best person for the job. He knew this company inside out. "How long are you talking?"

"I'm not sure. Another month or two perhaps."

He did his best to remain in his seat and not behave like the hotheaded teen he used to be. Was his father having second thoughts about Brandon heading the company? He was afraid to ask, but needed to know. Taking a deep, calming breath, he asked, "Are you thinking of putting someone else in the position?

"No."

Something—he didn't know what—in his father's tone gave Brandon pause. "Is that all?"

"Yes." His father released a deep sigh. "Son, I know you're upset, but I assure you this is just temporary."

Brandon stood and nodded. "Since it's almost five, I'm going to take off, unless you need me to stay."

He shook his head.

"Tell Mom hi."

"I will."

Brandon stalked back to his desk, locked up and set out for the gym his brother Khalil owned. The former model was now a highly sought-after personal trainer. With rush-hour traffic, it took Brandon nearly an hour to reach his destination, which incensed him even more. He was more than ready to take out his frustrations on the heavy bag.

"Damn, big brother. You might want to go easy on that bag."

Ignoring Khalil for the moment, Brandon continued with his punches. A few minutes later, winded, he removed his gloves, wiped his face with a towel and downed a bottle of water.

"Want to tell me what's going on and why you're about to dislodge my bag from the ceiling?"

He took up a position next to Khalil on the wall. "Dad is postponing his retirement. He said something came up that he needs to handle and it could be another couple of months."

"Why can't you handle it?"

"I offered, but he wouldn't even tell me what it was. It's bugging the hell out of me. I'm almost positive Uncle Thad is in on it, too." Brandon recalled the shared look between the two men.

Khalil swung his head in Brandon's direction. "I know he's not thinking about putting someone else in the CEO position. Granted, you do go over the top sometimes, like when that couple was trying to sue the company last year. You're lucky Siobhan and Morgan are still speaking to you."

He shot his brother a dark glare. "Shut up." When the accusations were first leveled, Siobhan, the company's PR director, had been out of town with her now husband and missed several calls that weekend. Their baby sister, Morgan, had been tasked to handle the legal case and, unbeknownst to the family, had become agent to a star football player. Both times, Brandon had confronted his sisters, feeling that they should have put the company first. Needless to say, it hadn't won him any brownie points. While Siobhan still worked for the company, Morgan had left the company six months ago and was doing well in the world of sports management. She had also married said football player. "Dad said he wasn't looking to place anyone else in the position, but I have a bad feeling about this."

"Thank God, because I'm certainly not going to do it, and neither is Malcolm." Their youngest brother, Morgan's twin, played professional football and had no interest in doing anything not sports-related. Khalil straightened from the wall. "Well, you've waited all this time for the position. Another few weeks won't kill you." Brandon grunted and Khalil laughed. "Besides, it'll give you more time to practice some patience."

Brandon grabbed his stuff and left Khalil standing there. He spent another forty-five minutes lifting weights before calling it a night. To add to his already foul mood, he realized that he'd forgotten to add a change of clothes and, after showering, had to put his wrinkled slacks and dress shirt back on. He spotted Khalil on his way out working with a client and threw up a wave.

At his car, Brandon tossed his gym bag in the backseat, then climbed in on the driver's side, started the engine and drove off. His stomach growled, letting him know it was far past the time for him to eat. As he merged onto the freeway, his cell rang and he engaged the Bluetooth device. "Hello."

"Brandon, can you stop by Thad's and pick up a folder for the meeting tomorrow morning?"

"Hey, Dad. I thought he was going to be there."

"He planned to, but the orthopedic clinic had a cancellation and can see him sooner than his original appointment two months from now."

Brandon knew how difficult it was to get an appointment with a specialist and understood the necessity of taking anything that came along earlier.

"I'd go, but your mother and I are on our way out and won't be back until late."

"I'll take care of it."

"Thanks. I'll see you in the morning."

Groaning, Brandon reversed his course and headed in the opposite direction. Twenty minutes later, he parked behind Uncle Thad's black Buick, got out and started up the walkway. Unlike the other houses on the block, this one had no steps leading to the door, which made it easier for him to maneuver his crutches or wheelchair. He rang the bell and, while waiting, scanned the meticulously groomed yard. Brandon remembered mowing it on many weekends growing up. The grass had turned brown in spots, but that was to be expected with the drought.

"Brandon, come on in."

He turned at the sound of his uncle's voice and stepped inside. "Hey, Unc. I see you still keep the yard looking good."

Uncle Thad smiled. "You know I wouldn't have it any other way." He adjusted his crutches and led the way farther into the house. "Sorry you had to go out of your way. I know you probably have things to do so I won't keep you." The inside of the house was just as neat, with not a speck of dust to be found anywhere, despite his bachelor-hood. He picked up a manila folder from the dining room table and handed it over.

"Thanks. Dad or I will fill you in when you get back." Brandon retraced his steps to the front door.

"All right. See you Friday."

He loped down the walk to his car, got in and backed out of the driveway. His stomach growled again. He had a steak marinating that he planned to grill and pair it with some potatoes and an ear of corn, but he was so hungry he didn't think he'd last the time it took to prepare the meal. But he didn't want to stop for fast food, either. The good thing was that Unc's house wasn't far from the free-way. He shifted his gaze from the road briefly to check the dash clock. Seven thirty. Hopefully, at this hour, he would have missed a good portion of the traffic. Brandon eased onto the highway and immediately saw that it was still a little heavy, but not too bad. His cell rang again. He sighed and connected.

"You were supposed to stop by my office and tell me what Dad wanted," Siobhan said as soon Brandon an-swered. "I went to your office and your assistant said that you left before five. You *never* leave before five. What happened?"

He sighed, not really wanting to talk about it. "I just thought I'd leave a little early today, Vonnie, that's all."

"Mm-hmm, and you didn't answer my question."

Rather than risk his sister coming to his house tonight—and she definitely would to get answers—Brandon gave in. "He's postponing his retirement." He repeated what he'd told Khalil.

"That's strange. Well, at least you'll still get the posi-tion."

"Yeah, but—" A truck cut across the highway and hit

something in the road that flew through the windshield of a car in the next lane a few lengths ahead. The car swerved and crashed into the center divide. Brandon let out a curse, flipped on his hazard lights and eased to a stop in front of the car. "There's an accident. I'll call you back."

Luckily, the shoulder was wide enough for the crashed car to be out of oncoming traffic. He jumped out, cell phone in hand and, being careful to stay closer to the shoulder, sprinted back to the passenger side of the car while dialing 911. He peered through the window and saw a woman inside. He gave the dispatcher the location and told him that the woman was conscious, but that a pipe of some sort was imbedded in her right shoulder. Brandon couldn't tell whether it had gone in deep or if it was just the deployed airbag holding it in place. "Miss, are you okay?" he called through the slightly open window.

She moaned, tried to push the airbag out of her face with her left hand and rolled her head in his direction. Her eyes fluttered closed and opened again.

In the fading sunlight, Brandon could see bits of glass in her hair and blood on her cheek where she had been cut. "Can you unlock the doors?" For a moment he thought she had passed out, then he heard the click of the lock. He opened the door and, being careful of all the glass on the seat, leaned in. "Help is on the way. What's your name?"

"Faith," she whispered.

"Faith, I'm Brandon. Are you hurt anywhere else besides your shoulder?"

"I… I don't know. Every…thing…hurts." Her eyes closed again.

"Faith, I need you to stay with me." He backed out and started to go around to the driver's side.

She moaned again. "Please…please don't leave."

"I'm just coming around to your side." He waited for a break in the traffic and hurried around to the driver's side.

Once there, he carefully opened the door and managed to give her some breathing room from the airbag. Brandon reached for her hand, his concern mounting. "Are you still with me?" She muttered something that sounded like yes. Brandon was momentarily distracted when another person approached.

"Is she okay, man? I called 911."

"Thanks. She's hanging in there." It seemed like an eternity passed before he heard the sirens. *Finally*.

When the paramedics and police arrived, Brandon stepped back. A police officer called him over to give a statement and his gaze kept straying to where the medical team was getting her out of the car and onto a gurney. Faith cried out and it took everything in him not to rush over. He finished his account and stood by watching with the other two people who had eventually stopped.

"Is one of you named Brandon?" a paramedic called out.

Brandon strode over. "Yeah. Me."

"She's asking for you."

He smiled down at her strapped down on the gurney. In the fading sunlight, he could see her face starting to swell where the airbag had hit her. "You're in good hands now."

"Thank you," Faith said, her voice barely audible. "My stuff…my…"

He took it to mean she wanted her things from the car. "I'll get them." To the paramedic he asked, "What hospital are you taking her to?" After getting the information, he walked back and retrieved her purse, keys and a small bag from the backseat. Why was he thinking about going to the hospital? He'd done his civic duty. It would be easy to hand off her belongings to one of the officers and be on his way. But for some reason, he needed to make sure— for himself—that she was okay. Brandon slid behind the wheel of his car and, instead of going home, merged back onto the freeway and headed to the hospital.

Chapter 2

Faith slowly came awake in a semidark room and it took her a moment for her to register where she was. She'd had the most awesome dream about a handsome guardian angel. Too bad it was just a dream. Never would she be so lucky as to run across a man like him. She lifted her hand and pain shot through her right shoulder and flared out to every part of her body. She sucked in a sharp breath and eased her hand down. She went still at the sight of a man asleep in a chair. She frowned. *Who in the world...?* As if sensing her scrutiny, he opened his eyes and pushed up from the chair. Faith blinked. He was even taller than she originally thought, well-built and easily the most handsome man she'd seen in a long time.

"Hey," he said softly.

"I thought I dreamt you."

His deep chuckle filled the room. "No. I'm very real."

Faith tried to clear the cobwebs from her mind. "You

helped me when I crashed." She thought for a moment. "Brandon?"

He nodded. "How are you feeling?"

"Everything hurts. Even breathing hurts." She closed her eyes briefly. "Um…what time is it?" she murmured.

Brandon checked his watch. "A little after eleven."

"You've been here all this time?"

"For the most part. I brought your stuff and I didn't want to leave it with anyone without your permission." He placed them on the tray.

"Thank you."

"Do you want me to call your husband or family?"

Faith wanted to roll her eyes at the husband reference, but just the thought made her ache, so she settled for saying, "I'm not married."

"What about family—Mom, Dad?"

The last person she wanted to talk to was her mother. "My parents don't live here," she added softly. She had been on her way to her father's house, but chickened out before arriving and had turned around to go back to the hotel when she'd had the accident.

A frown creased his brow. "You don't have anyone here?"

"No. I live in Oregon. I just got here yesterday."

"Hell of a welcome."

"Tell me about it," she muttered.

"Well, now that I know you're okay, I'm going to leave. I'll stop by to see you tomorrow to make sure you don't need anything." Brandon covered her uninjured hand with his large one and gave it a gentle squeeze.

Despite every inch of her body aching, the warmth of his touch sent an entirely different sensation flowing through her. The intense way he was staring at her made her think he had felt something, as well.

"I…um…" Brandon eased his hand from hers. "Get

some rest." However, he didn't move, his interest clear as glass. After another moment he walked to the door, but turned back once more. "Good night."

"Good night." Faith watched as he slipped out the door, her heart still racing. Her life seemed to be a mess right now, but knowing she would see Brandon again made her smile.

The next morning Faith was coherent enough to think. But the nurse had just given her more pain medication and she needed to call Kathi before it kicked in, to let her know about the accident. She dug inside her purse and pulled out her cell.

"Hey, girl," Kathi said when she answered. "Have you seen your father yet?"

"I didn't get a chance. I had an accident last night on the freeway." She shared the details of what happened.

"Oh, my God! I'm taking the first flight out," Kathi said before Faith could finish. "What hospital are you in?"

"Kathi, you don't need to come down here. Luckily, the windshield deflected the momentum of the pipe and the wound isn't too deep. My face stings from the cuts and it's swollen where the airbag hit me. They said I have a mild concussion and that's why they're keeping me. I'll be fine." Her friend was a natural-born worrywart and, if she came to town, would stand over Faith like a mother hen guarding her chicks until Faith was completely healed.

"When are you going home?"

"The doctor said most likely tomorrow."

"Fine. I'll be there Saturday morning. That'll give you a day to get settled into the hotel. Do your parents know?"

"I talked to my dad and he said he'd tell my mother." Faith had called her stepfather purposely because she didn't want to run the risk of hearing her mother say, "I told you nothing good could come from you going to visit that man."

"What about your biological father?"

"How would it look if I called him out of the blue and said, 'Hi, I'm your long lost daughter, and oh, by the way, I was in a car accident. Can you come take care of me?' No, I'll wait until I'm better."

"Why? He's the one who extended the invitation. I'm sure he'd be okay with it."

"But I'm not."

"If you say so. What about the car and your stuff?"

"I'll call the rental company after I get out of the hospital to deal with the car. Thankfully, I got the insurance. But a really nice guy stopped on the side of the road and stayed with me until the paramedics came and brought my stuff to the hospital."

"You were lucky. What did he look like?"

"The man is drop-dead fine, over six feet, muscles and has the greatest smile." Rich walnut skin, nutmeg-colored eyes and a voice smooth as velvet…definitely sexy.

Kathi laughed. "I see the accident didn't affect your eyesight."

Faith chuckled, then moaned. "Oh, don't make me laugh."

"Sorry. I'm hanging up so you can get some rest. I'll call you tomorrow to let you know what time my flight gets in."

"Sounds good. These pain meds are kicking in and I'm feeling dizzy again." She told Kathi when she thought she'd be at the hotel and ended the call. Gradually, the throbbing pain in her shoulder started to dull, as did the other aches in her body. Her mind went back to Thaddeus Whitcomb. Rather than tell him she would visit, she had decided to come to town and drive by his house with the hopes of catching a glimpse of him first. Would he really be as glad to see her as his letters indicated or was her mother right—that she should leave it alone? Faith had to figure out what to do about him, find another car and a whole slew of other things, but at the moment, she just needed to sleep.

"Hey, Justin," Brandon said to his brother-in-law Thursday morning. "Have a seat."

Justin took the proffered chair. "Siobhan said you wanted to talk to me."

"I wanted to see how the tests were going and find out when you think the system will be ready to go." Justin had partnered with the company to manufacture his in-home alert system. With the use of sensors placed around the home, real-time data could be sent directly to a smartphone from a wireless hub—whether a door had been left open, a stove left on, or if a person hadn't moved in hours—that allowed elderly relatives to remain at home and gave caregivers peace of mind.

"I want to do a few more tests before running the consumer trials. If all goes well, maybe six months or so."

Brandon sighed. "That long?"

"I'd rather work out as many bugs in the system before it hits the market than risk putting it out there and failing."

"You're right. I'm just anxious."

Justin laughed. "Yeah, so am I. Oh, Siobhan told me about you stopping to help some people in an accident last night. Are they okay?"

"It was just one woman and she's going to be okay. A truck hit a pipe in the road and it went through her windshield. She crashed into the divider. The pipe caught her in the shoulder, but it didn't do as much damage as it could have."

"Whoa. What are the chances of something that freaky happening?"

"I know, right? The kicker is she doesn't live here and had just gotten to town Tuesday."

"Not a good way to start a trip. If I were her, I might not want to visit LA again," he said with a wry chuckle and stood up.

"True that."

"If you're not busy, you can come over for dinner. Siobhan and I are planning to grill some salmon."

"Thanks for the offer, but I told Faith I would stop by to check on her."

"Who's Faith?"

"The woman from the accident." And the one who'd kept him up all night thinking about her.

A slow smile spread across Justin's lips. "Well now."

Brandon shook his head. "It's nothing like that. She doesn't know anyone in town and I'm just being neighborly. If it were Siobhan or Morgan, I'd want someone to do the same for them if they happened to be hurt and alone."

Justin nodded. "I hear you. I'd want the same for Yvonne and Jocelyn."

Brandon knew Justin would understand since he had two younger sisters.

"I'll see you later."

After Justin exited, he turned his attention back to work, but Faith was never far from his thoughts. True, he was being friendly, but something about her intrigued him. He hadn't been able to get her beautiful face out of his mind since leaving her last night.

Brandon managed to finish going through and signing all the documents his assistant had left by late afternoon. For the second day in a row, he was packed up and ready to leave at closing time. Most evenings, he didn't leave until seven or eight, not late enough for his father to fuss, but still late. Nolan Gray believed in working hard, but he also tried to teach his five children that there was more to life than work and sometimes had to force Brandon and Siobhan out of the office at a decent hour. Brandon worked hard, but he did make time to play on occasion. Although lately, he'd been more focused on work.

By leaving at five thirty, Brandon ended up right in the middle of rush-hour traffic. It took him more than an hour to get to the hospital, a drive that would have normally been twenty minutes. He parked in the lot and entered the lobby. Passing the gift shop, he saw several floral bouquets lining the window. On an impulse, he ducked inside and bought one, surprising himself. He usually steered clear of those types of sentiments because he didn't want women to read anything into the gesture.

He took the elevator to her floor and poked his head in the door. Seeing that Faith was awake, he walked fully into the room. "Hi. These are for you." He placed them on the small table.

Faith's eyes lit up. "Hi, and thank you. They're beautiful."

The smile she gave Brandon warmed him all over and made him glad that he had purchased them. "How are you feeling today?"

"My face still stings from all the cuts and being hit by the airbag, my shoulder hurts like crazy and my body is sore. But, it could've been worse so I'm grateful."

His gaze roamed over her face. He hadn't imagined her beauty. Even with the small abrasions, her ebony skin looked soft to the touch and he stifled the urge to stroke a finger down her cheek to find out. "Has the doctor said how long they're keeping you?"

"She said I can go home tomorrow afternoon sometime."

"You said you got into town on Tuesday. Where are you staying?"

"I booked a room at one of those extended stay hotels near the airport."

"So that means you'll be here for a little while." He didn't know why the prospect of her being around longer made him happy.

"Yes. I have some business to take care of and I don't know how long it will take."

"By the looks of your car, you'll have to get another one."

"It's a rental, and that's one more thing to add to my growing list. Weird things happen, I'm learning, so I plan to take it one step at a time."

"How are you getting home tomorrow?"

Faith shrugged. "Probably take a cab."

"I'll pick you up," Brandon said without thought. He'd never taken off work for a woman. Ever. But the moment the words left his mouth, they felt right.

"You don't have to do that, Brandon. You've been very nice and I appreciate everything you've done, but I don't want to impose on you."

"It's no trouble, Faith. You're still healing and in a new city. You shouldn't have to worry about trying to figure out transportation, as well."

"I don't want to disrupt your family time."

"My family gets together about once a month at my parents' house…on a Sunday. I don't have any other commitments. To anyone." Brandon held her gaze, wanting her to understand exactly what he meant. True, he wanted to make sure she got settled safely, but he also wanted to see her again and learn more about her. Aside from her beauty, he was drawn to her smile and positive attitude despite her current circumstances. He probably would have been as grouchy as a bear if their places were switched.

"Oh."

He smiled. "I'll be here around one in case they let you out earlier. Do you have a number where I can call you?"

"I have my cell."

Brandon pulled out his phone and inputted the numbers she recited. "Let me give you mine in case you need something before I get here." She opened her phone to the contacts, he added his name and number and handed it back. Their hands brushed and he felt the same spark he had the night before, which made him all the more curious. Sure he dated when it suited him but Brandon couldn't explain this attraction. It was…different.

Faith lifted a brow. "Are you sure you can take off work? I don't want to cause you problems with your job."

He opened his mouth to tell her that technically he was the boss, but changed his mind. Not that he'd put Faith in the same category, but since he had been appointed director of the safety division three years ago, women tended to be more attracted to the money they thought he made than him. His last long-term relationship ended when his girlfriend became angry because Brandon refused to give her two brothers jobs in management with a hefty salary, despite the fact that neither man had a college degree or had ever worked in a company such as theirs. After that, he kept his job and title to himself. "It won't be a problem. I have enough leave time accumulated to give every employee a week off." That much was true. He rarely took days off, and his father forced him to take at least one week off for vacation yearly.

She laughed. "Must be nice."

The warm sound of her laugh elicited a strange stirring in his gut. "It is."

The nurse came in with Faith's dinner, placed it on the tray and positioned it in front of her. When Faith said she didn't need anything else, the woman departed with a smile.

Faith lifted the dome and wrinkled her nose. "Ugh. I'll be glad to get out of here and get some real food."

Brandon laughed. "When you're better, maybe we can go out for dinner or something so you can get that *real food*. That is if it doesn't interfere with your business."

She gave him a shy smile. "I'd like that."

He wanted to stay and talk to her, but knew she needed to rest. "You should eat your dinner before it gets cold."

"Gee, thanks," she said with a chuckle, glancing at the tray. "That dinner can't come soon enough."

Looking down at the plate filled with shriveled green beans, dry mashed potatoes and some kind of meat smothered in brown gravy, he agreed. "Yeah."

"You're welcome to join me."

"I would, but I had a late lunch." In reality, he'd barely stopped for lunch and was starving. But not enough to voluntarily eat hospital food.

"Coward."

"You've got that right."

Faith winced.

"Pain coming back?"

She closed her eyes for a moment. "Yep."

"I didn't mean to stay so long," Brandon said with concern.

"You didn't. You helped me forget about the pain for a few minutes," she added softly.

Their eyes held for a lengthy moment. "Do you want me to get the nurse?"

"I have the call button right here." She pressed it and moments later a nurse entered.

"What can I get for you?" the nurse asked.

"The pain is back with a vengeance," Faith said.

"On a scale of one to ten, how would you rate it?"

"Nine and a half."

Brandon stood off to the side while the nurse checked

to see when Faith had medication last. She retrieved the pills from a locked cabinet, placed them in a small cup and handed them to Faith, along with some water.

"Thank you."

The nurse took the cup, tossed it into the trash and departed.

"That's my cue," Brandon said. "I'll see you tomorrow." Unable to resist, he reached for her hand, wanting to touch her again, and placed a soft kiss on the back. Her gaze flew to his. Had she felt the same current flowing as he did?

She eased her hand back. "Good night, Brandon, and thanks for stopping by."

"Good night." Brandon told himself he wasn't in the market for a relationship and he needed to put a tight rein on whatever was happening between them, regardless of their mutual attraction. Besides, Faith didn't live in LA and long-distance relationships had never been on his list. However, he had agreed to take her to dinner, but that was it. One dinner. Nothing else.

Chapter 3

"Got a minute, Dad?" Brandon said, entering his father's office Friday.

"Of course." As usual, his shirtsleeves were still down and his tie tightened. The man seemed to never break a sweat.

He glanced around the space that would be his, hopefully soon, and took the chair on the other side of the large mahogany desk. "You mind if I take off for the rest of the day?"

His father checked his watch and lifted a brow. "You coming down with something?"

"No," he answered with a chuckle.

"It's noon, Brandon. I can't remember one time that you've left this early. Actually, I don't think you ever have. Most times I have to threaten to have security remove you."

"That's cold, Dad. Anyway, I promised to help a friend."

His dad smiled. "Go ahead. You need to take some

time off anyhow. And you know you don't really have to ask, son."

"Thanks. What's going on with that problem?"

His smile faded and he turned slightly to stare out of the large window that took up almost an entire wall. "There's no change. We need to give it another two or three weeks before deciding anything."

"You always said that I'm pretty good at negotiating, so like I said before, I'd be happy to help speed things up."

Facing, Brandon, he said, "Not all things can be done that way, Brandon. Just be patient and enjoy your afternoon off."

Sighing inwardly, Brandon nodded. "See you on Monday." Patience had never been his strong suit and, at thirty-three, he didn't think he'd ever develop the virtue. He stopped at home first to change into shorts and T-shirt, still bothered by his father's words. His father had assured him that nothing would change pertaining to Brandon assuming the role of CEO. But Brandon couldn't rid himself of the nagging feeling that whatever was going on would impact him. And in a big way. However, by the time he made it to the hospital, his thoughts had shifted to Faith. He had enjoyed talking with her last night and was uncharacteristically excited to see her. Shaking it off, he tried to tell himself he was just being friendly. Yet, there wasn't anything friendly about the sensations that spread through him when she greeted him with her amazing smile. Brandon did his best to ignore them.

"Hi, Brandon."

"Hello, yourself. I see you're all ready." She had on the same pants she wore the day of the accident and one of the short hospital gowns. He assumed her top had been ruined in the accident.

Faith frowned. "More than ready to get out of these

clothes, take a real shower and do something with this hair."

He smiled inwardly at Faith's attempt to smooth down the straight, shoulder-length strands as best she could.

"I've already signed the discharge papers, but I need to stop at a pharmacy to fill the prescription."

"I'm sure we can find one on the way to the hotel. Is there anywhere else you need to stop?"

She sighed. "Yes. I didn't get a chance to go grocery shopping, so if we can find a store, too, I'd appreciate it."

"Sure."

A nurse came in with a wheelchair and asked Brandon to meet them at the entrance.

He took her bag and the flowers, retrieved his car and pulled into the circle driveway in front of the door. He had the door open and waiting when Faith appeared. Seeing the difficulty she had getting in, Brandon was glad he'd decided to drive his car rather than his truck. She would not have been able to climb into the cab with her injured shoulder.

Brandon reached in and carefully fastened her seat belt. "Is that too tight?" She lifted her head and their faces were mere inches apart. The air between them shifted.

"No. It's…it's fine."

His gaze dropped to her gorgeous mouth. Would her lips be as soft as they looked? Her eyes widened and he heard her sharp intake of breath. *What am I doing?* He straightened, closed the door and went around to the driver's side.

"Um, so where are we going first?" Faith asked as he exited the lot.

"I thought we'd drop off your prescription. It may take a while to fill. We can go to the store to pick up whatever you need while we wait." Since her hotel was near the airport, he figured he'd find a pharmacy and grocery store somewhere along Century Boulevard.

"Can we stop at the hotel before going shopping? I really need a shower." She gave him the name and street of the hotel.

"No problem." As he drove, Brandon stole glances at Faith. He could tell she was still in pain so he didn't offer any conversation. She sat with her head against the seat, eyes closed, and he noticed that she grimaced every now and again. When they reached the drugstore, the pharmacist told them the prescription would be ready in an hour, which gave them plenty of time to finish the other errands. He drove to the hotel and parked as close as he could to her unit.

Faith groaned when they arrived. "I forgot about the stairs." Her room was on the second floor and the elevator in this particular section of the complex was out of order.

"Just take your time and I'll carry everything up." Once inside, Brandon debated whether to wait in the car or the room. He didn't want either of them to be uncomfortable. But his protective side won out. "If it's okay with you, I'll wait here in the living room in case you need help."

She stared at him for a long moment, and then said softly, "Thank you."

A few minutes later, he heard water running and tried his best not to think about Faith naked with the water streaming down her body. He'd gotten the first glimpse of her shapely bottom in those clingy knit pants when she walked up the stairs in front of him, reminding him just how long it had been since his last sexual encounter. He scrubbed a hand down his face. First he was thinking about kissing her and now imagining how it would feel to run his hands over her body. "Get it together," he muttered.

Putting sensual thoughts of Faith out of his mind, Brandon fished out his cell and checked his work emails. He opened one from the marketing department providing him with an update on how the bath rails were doing. After the lawsuit last year where a couple claimed one of the rails had broken and resulted in injury to the man's elderly wife, the numbers had gone down. Morgan had taken the lead on the case and proved their company hadn't been at fault, and now things were finally starting to turn around.

"I'm ready, Brandon."

Brandon's head popped up at the sound of Faith's voice and he came to his feet swiftly. She had on another pair of knit pants and a loose top that buttoned down the front. She'd brushed her hair back and secured it with a headband. Her face wasn't as swollen and the cuts appeared to be healing. "Feel better?"

"Much," Faith answered with a smile. "Although, it took some serious maneuvering to shower and get dressed."

They made another careful trip down the stairs to the car and he drove her to the store. As they shopped, her steps grew slower and slower. "How about you just get enough to last for the first few days or so?" he suggested. "That way you can go back to the hotel and lay down. You look like you're fading fast."

She gave him a wan smile. "Who would've thought I'd be ready to quit shopping after ten minutes?" She glanced over at the basket Brandon carried. "That should hold me until I'm able to get back." At the register, Faith let out a frustrated sigh. "Brandon, can you please hold my purse open so I can get my wallet?"

He did as she asked and helped her slide the card. "I take it you're right handed."

"Yes. The only thing I can do with my left hand is type. This is a mess."

Brandon chuckled softly as he bagged the groceries. The drive back to the drugstore and the hotel took less than twenty minutes. He set her bags on the counter in the kitchen. "Do you want me to put this stuff away for you?"

Faith angled her head. "If you could just take care of

the things that need to be refrigerated, I'd appreciate it. I'll put the rest away later."

"Okay. You should probably take one of those pain pills." He opened the container and a bottle of water for her and started putting the food away.

"Thanks." She swallowed the tablet and stood off to the side.

Brandon checked the bags to make sure he hadn't missed anything. "I think that's it. I opened a few bottles of the water and left the caps loosened for you, same with your medicine." With the difficulties she'd had getting her wallet out, he wondered how she would manage to cook using her left hand, but didn't ask. It wasn't his business. *It's not like I'm going to cook for her.*

"Brandon, I don't know how I'll ever be able to repay you for your kindness." Faith came up on tiptoe and kissed his cheek. "I'm grateful for all your help."

The warmth and softness of her lips against his skin sent a slow burn through his body. The desire to turn his head into the kiss rose sharply and almost blazed past his carefully constructed defenses. She admittedly intrigued him, but this attraction had blindsided him and seemed to be stronger than what he had experienced with any woman in his past. He took a couple of steps to put some distance between them. "I'm glad I could help. Be sure to let me know how you're doing. And when you're ready, we can have that dinner."

"I will." She walked him to the door and an awkward silence ensued. She gave his hand a squeeze. "I'll see you later."

"Take care of yourself, Faith." He reluctantly released her hand and, just like before, had a hard time getting his feet to move. Finally he forced himself to leave. She lifted her hand in a wave and gave him a smile that had his heart beating a little faster. A slow grin spread across his lips.

His smile was still in place by the time he made it home. He hadn't gone out on a date in months due to his work schedule, and because he needed a break from the drama of relationships. But thinking about going out with Faith filled him with a strange kind of anticipation. She said she only planned to be here for a short while, plenty of time for some fun. He could work with that. Then there was that kiss. The remembrance of her lips against his cheek stayed on his mind for the remainder of the day. He knew right then he might be in trouble.

Faith awakened from a two-hour nap feeling a little better, glad that the medication had done its job. She went into the kitchen to make something to eat, but any movement of her right arm or hand caused a searing pain. She initially tried some yogurt, but eating with her left hand proved more of a challenge than she'd thought. After several frustrating minutes, she settled for a slice of cheese and saltine crackers. She went to the refrigerator for something to drink and found that not only had Brandon opened the bottles of water, but also the carton of orange juice. She sent up a silent thank-you. What she wouldn't give to have a man like him in her life—fine, sexy and a gentleman all rolled up in one. Today had been her first chance to see him in something other than a dress shirt and slacks. Just like everything else about him, his lean, muscular body was impressive. Memories of his biceps flexing as he opened the bottles of water flashed in her mind. *It's just my luck that the one time I meet a nice man he lives in a totally different state.* Faith shook her head. She took her juice to the small dining table, came back for the crackers and cheese and took a seat.

While munching on her snack, her gaze strayed to the box of letters across the room. Automatically, her thoughts shifted to the man who was supposed to be her father. And again she questioned how different her life might have been with him in it. Outside of the letter she'd read the day she received the box, Faith hadn't gotten up the nerve to read more for fear of what she would find.

Now, however, curiosity propelled her across the room and she took out the letters. She decided to start with the newest, thinking it would give her a clear picture of Thaddeus Whitcomb now. It took some maneuvering, but she managed to get the envelope open and the paper out.

My Darling Daughter,
I have not given up hope that I will one day hold you in my arms again. I hope this letter reaches you and finds you well. Know that I have never stopped trying to find you and will always love you. Please feel free to contact me or visit whenever you like.
Dad

He had included his address and telephone number. Tears misted her eyes. She laid it aside and picked up one that had been written twenty-eight years ago, when she was two. He had been stationed in Germany and included a picture of himself wearing his army uniform. Faith studied his handsome dark features and realized she looked a lot like him. For a while, she read more letters. In each, he always described the place and what was going on. She smiled at his sense of humor. All of the letters ended with him telling her how much he loved her and couldn't wait to see her. Swiping at her tears, Faith became angry with her mother all over again. Her mother made it seem as though her father had come back as some sort of a monster, yet Faith only saw a man who had been denied the privilege of knowing his daughter. While she acknowledged that she didn't know a lot about PTSD, by the tone of his letters, it seemed like her father had learned to cope well.

She picked up the picture of him holding her again and felt her emotions rising. Growing up, whenever she'd asked her mother about her father, she'd received the same answer each time—he'd died when she was two and no, there were no pictures. The pain in her heart swelled and she put the letters aside and went back to lie down. She tried listening to music and reading at first, but it didn't help. Finally, she turned on the television and surfed through the channels, looking for anything that would take her mind off the myriad feelings bombarding her. In the end, she gave up. Her head hurt, the pain in her shoulder increased and she was starving.

Faith ate a handful of almonds, drank more water and snacked on a few grapes, but she needed something of substance. She thought about going out briefly before remembering she didn't have a car. She didn't have time for this. Her cell rang, interrupting her mental tirade.

"Hello."

"Hey, girlfriend. Are you home yet?"

"Hey, Kathi. Yeah, I got home about three hours ago."

"Glad to hear it. I get in tomorrow at noon and I'm staying until Monday. What's the name of the hotel where you're staying? I need to book a room."

"No need. I have an extra bed." She gave Kathi her room number and the hotel's address.

"Even better. That way I can keep an eye on you. Do I need to stop and pick up groceries and stuff before I get there?"

"I have some food here." Faith opened her mouth to say that she couldn't cook with one arm, but decided against it. Kathi would change her flight in a heartbeat and be on the next plane out. "But we can go shopping for whatever you need once you arrive. There's a grocery store a few miles away."

"Okay. Is there anything you want from your place?"

Faith had asked Kathi to check on her house until Faith returned.

"I don't think so, but if I think of something later tonight, I'll text you."

"All right. See you tomorrow and make sure you rest."

Faith laughed softly. "Yes, Mother." They talked a minute longer and hung up.

Faith's stomach growled. *Back to the task of finding food.* Determined to make it work, she pulled out a small skillet, butter and an egg. How hard could it be to scramble an egg with one hand? Five minutes later, she had her answer. She could stir the egg in the pan, but had difficulty scooping it out. As a result, she ended up burning most of it. Faith stared at the hard, brown bits on her plate and frowned. Sighing heavily, she dumped the inedible mess down the garbage disposal, set the pan in the sink and trudged back to the bedroom.

An hour later, a knock sounded. The clock on the nightstand read eight o'clock. *Maybe housekeeping.* She sat up gingerly, scooted off the bed and walked out to the front. She looked through the peephole and was surprised to see Brandon standing there. She quickly undid the locks and opened the door. "Brandon, hey. What are you doing here?" He had on a pair of basketball shorts and T-shirt that outlined his muscular chest and washboard abs.

He unleashed that mesmerizing smile and held up a white bag. "Thought you'd might have some trouble cooking."

Faith sighed in relief. "Bless you. Come in."

Brandon chuckled. "Sounds like you're happy to see me."

"You have no idea. Please tell me that what you have in that bag doesn't require me to use a spoon and I'll name my firstborn after you."

His laughter filled the room. "Brandon *is* a nice name."

He carried the bag over to the table, took out a disposable container and opened it. "I didn't know what you liked, so I took a chance on a club sandwich and French fries. Hope that's okay."

She wanted to throw her arms around his neck and kiss him. "More than okay. Thank you."

He sniffed and surveyed the room. "Were you trying to cook?"

"Yeah. I thought it would be easy to scramble an egg. It was. But by the time I could get it out of the pan with my left hand, it no longer resembled something edible."

His eyebrows shot up. "You haven't eaten anything since I left you?"

"I had a slice of cheese, five crackers, a handful of almonds and some grapes." She shrugged. "It was the best I could do."

"Then I'm glad I stopped by."

"Me, too." They fell silent.

"Well, I only came to drop off the food, so…and I really wanted to see you again."

His soft confession made her pulse skip. And, truthfully, she had wanted to see him, too. Before she could talk herself out of all the reasons it would be a bad idea to spend more with him, she said, "Then why don't you stay and keep me company."

Brandon smiled. "I'd love to." He seated her and took the adjacent chair.

Faith recited a quick blessing and started in on the sandwich. She was so hungry she devoured the first half in a matter of a few bites. She lifted her head and saw Brandon staring at her with faint amusement. "Oh, I'm sorry. Do you want some?"

"No, thank you. I've already eaten. I'm just glad you're enjoying my selections." He leaned forward and braced his arm on the table. "What else do you enjoy?"

She paused with a fry halfway to her mouth. "I like reading, shopping and designing websites."

"Quite an eclectic mix," he said with a laugh.

"Hey, what can I say?" She ate another fry. Belatedly, she remembered she hadn't gotten anything to drink. When she made a move to stand, Brandon jumped to his feet to help her.

"Do you need something?"

"I was just going to get some water or juice."

"Sit down. I'll get it."

Her brow lifted and she lowered herself back down. "Kind of bossy, aren't you?"

"One of my more stellar traits, I'm afraid." Brandon retrieved a glass from the cabinet. "Which one, water or juice?"

"I'll take the juice, please." Faith continued to eat and thanked him when he placed the glass in front of her. Silence rose between them and he seemed content to just sit and watch her. Any other time, she would have felt uncomfortable with someone staring at her while she ate, but not today. Today, she was too hungry to care. As soon as she finished, he rose from the table, cleaned up and discarded the empty container. Faith had never been around a man like him and couldn't believe some woman hadn't snatched him up. At the hospital, he'd said he didn't have a commitment to anyone. There had to be something wrong with the women in this city. Or maybe it was him. "So, any big plans tonight?"

"Just catching up on some work."

Faith was instantly contrite. He'd taken off half his workday for her. She got up and walked over to where he still stood in the utility kitchen. "I'm sorry. You took off work for me and now you have to spend your Friday evening working. By the way, what do you do?"

He hesitated briefly. "I work for a home safety company. And, believe me, whether I'd worked half a day or a full one, my evening would have been spent doing the same thing. Actually, you've helped me out by allowing me to hang out with you tonight."

She leaned against the counter. His abrupt answer made her wonder if he was having problems at his job. "Why *are* you helping me? Not that I don't appreciate it, but, I mean, you've gone far above the 'good Samaritan' role."

Brandon folded his arms across his wide chest and angled his head thoughtfully. "You're a beautiful woman, no getting around that. But you have a great personality and a way about you that intrigues me. I like you, Faith. It's as simple as that."

"Um…wow. Okay. You're very direct."

His voice dipped an octave and his gaze trapped her. "Always."

The heat swirled around them. To cover her nervousness, she took a step back and cleared her throat. "Well, I don't want to be responsible for you being up all night, so…"

"Yeah. I'd better go." Yet neither of them moved. After several charged moments, Brandon moved around her and walked toward the door.

Faith followed. "Good night, Brandon. And thank you again…for everything."

"You're welcome." He turned the knob and paused.

Before she could blink, he bent and covered her mouth in a kiss so sweet it made her eyes close and her heart flip.

"Good night, Faith." And he was gone.

Faith leaned against the door. She had come to LA for one reason and one reason only, and she would do well to keep that in the forefront of her mind. But thinking of that kiss, she guessed it might be harder than she'd expected.

Chapter 4

Brandon was up at six Saturday morning, sitting in his home office going over reports. Thoughts of Faith had plagued him all night long and made it difficult for him to sleep, so he'd decided to make good use of his time. He came across a report from Khalil. His brother wanted specialized equipment for people with low vision or blindness. He picked up the phone to call.

"What's up, big brother?" Khalil said when he answered.

"Hey. Just came across your report. You're looking to add more equipment?"

"Actually, I want to create an area in the gym to put machines that have braille on the plates and install a special type of flooring that feels like a mat, but without the uneven surface."

"Where do you come up with these ideas?" Khalil already had designated areas set up for individuals with disabilities, from wheelchairs that reclined flat to allow a person to lie under a weight bench, to machines that accommodated amputees comfortably.

Khalil chuckled. "My mind is always working, but I had a client with low vision and she mentioned there not being any gyms that allowed her to work out without a trainer, so I asked her what kinds of equipment she thought would be useful, added my own ideas and voilà. I have some sketches of what I want and can show them to you when you get here. You are still coming?"

"Yeah, I'll be there." Brandon and his brothers got together once or twice a month to play basketball and work out. The game had expanded to include his two brothers-in-law. Khalil typically played as a substitute or when he had time. "I'll get there about half an hour earlier, if you're available."

"I can do that. I don't have a client until later this afternoon."

"I'll see you then." Brandon disconnected and finished reading through and making notes on the other reports.

The gym was crowded, as it was usually on a Saturday. He headed directly for Khalil's upstairs office and knocked on the partially open door.

Khalil looked away from his computer. "Come on in. Let me finish logging in these fitness testing results and we can talk."

Brandon took the chair across from the desk and nodded.

A few minutes later, Khalil retrieved a manila folder from a locked file cabinet and handed it to Brandon. "These sketches are still pretty rough. I'll have better ones when I get ready to submit to the design team. I already purchased a handheld braille labeler, but I want the plates to be shaped differently so they'll be a little more user-friendly with the labels." He pointed out the details of each.

"You know you could have gone the art route." Along

with being a model and fitness buff, his brother was also a skilled artist.

Khalil shook his head and made a face. "No way. I didn't want to get stuck having to draw fruit, abstracts I don't understand and other crap I can't stand. I'd rather draw or paint what I want." He favored landscapes and people, but could also draw vehicles and, apparently, gym equipment.

Brandon laughed. "Well, just let me know when you're ready and I'll set up a meeting. Is this only for the second gym?"

"No. I'm rearranging some of the equipment here to create a space, as well. With two floors, I have a little flexibility."

Brandon stood. "Okay. Are you playing today?"

"I don't know. I have a few things I need to finish, but I may poke my head in the door. Are Malcolm and Omar coming?"

"I got a text from Malcolm yesterday and he said he'd be here. I'm guessing he talked to Omar."

"Dad say anything else about when you'll take over?"

"No."

"What are y'all old men doing up here? We playing ball or what?"

Brandon and Khalil turned to find Malcolm standing in the door. Brandon said, "Who are you calling old?" He noticed Omar, Morgan's husband, standing off to the side chuckling. "What's up, Omar?"

"It's all good," Omar said, entering the office and doing a fist bump with Brandon and Khalil.

The men filed out of the office and went downstairs to the basketball court. They shot around while waiting for Justin to arrive.

"Do you think the Cobras will take it all again this

year?" Khalil asked Malcolm and Omar. The LA Cobras football team had won the championship last season.

Omar sank a jump shot. "I think we have a good chance to repeat."

"We still have our key offensive and defensive weapons, and my brother over here," Malcolm said, gesturing to Omar, "is moving to the wide receiver position permanently this year. With Marcus Dupree at receiver on the right, we've got the two best in the league. Of course, with me at running back, what do you expect?"

Brandon shook his head. "No shame in your game, I see."

Malcolm shrugged. "I learned from my big brothers."

"What's up, good people?" Justin strolled over to where the other men were and they went through another round of greetings. "Are we playing Horse today, since there are five of us?"

"That'll work," Brandon said. "Although, if you miss as many shots as last time, you'll be spelling *horse* and out of the game before we go around two times." They all laughed.

"Ha-ha, funny. Just toss me the damn ball."

"I think I'm gonna help my brother-in-law out today," Khalil said. "I have to get back to the office, so you can play a little two-on-two. Go easy on him," he added, causing the men to laugh harder. "It's that married thing." He shuddered.

Omar lifted a brow. "You have something against being married?"

"Hell, yeah. Too many beautiful ladies, so little time. I'll check y'all later," he called over his shoulder as he left.

Malcolm chuckled. "He does have a point. I say you married men team up and let us single brothers show you a little somethin' somethin'."

Brandon folded his arms. "Unless you're scared."

Justin and Omar shared a look, and Justin said, "Let's go."

In the first few minutes of the game, Brandon and Malcolm went up four to nothing. Brandon tossed the ball to Omar to take it out. "Guess it's true that once you're married you lose some of your skills."

Omar passed the ball to Justin, who threw it up toward the basket where Omar dunked it. "On the contrary, we haven't lost anything."

The trash talking continued and Justin and Omar pulled ahead, needing one point to win. Justin laughed. "Looks like the *married* men are conducting the lessons today, right, Omar?"

"True that, my brother."

"Quit talking and play ball," Brandon groused.

"Gladly," Omar said, dribbling the ball twice and sinking a shot from three-point range. He let out a whoop and he and Justin high-fived. "Guess we won't be needing that consolation prize today."

Justin laughed. "Maybe you two ought to try marriage... get rid of some of that aggression and tension. I can't tell you how relaxed I've been since marrying Siobhan. There's nothing like waking up beside that one special woman every day."

Omar smiled and nodded. "Amen."

Malcolm waved them off. "Whatever. I'll pass."

Brandon didn't comment. Hearing Justin and Omar talk affectionately about their wives—not like he expected them to say anything less about his sisters—automatically made Brandon think of Faith. *Why am I thinking about her? I am* not *looking to get married anytime soon.* But he couldn't help it. How was she managing with her injuries? Had she gotten another car? Was she eating enough? And would she let him kiss her again? His mind said he needed some space, especially after the unexpected sensations he'd felt when kissing her. He couldn't get the feel of her kiss out of his mind and wanted to do it again, leisurely this time, until he got his fill.

"Brandon."

Malcolm's voice broke into his musings. "What?"

"I asked if you were coming with us to Omar's parents' restaurant for lunch."

Brandon hesitated. "Nah, not today. I have something I need to take care of." He met Justin's knowing smile. "I'll catch you guys next time."

"Must be pretty important," Justin said with a glint of amusement in his eyes as they headed for the showers.

"Yeah, something like that." Justin had been the only person Brandon had mentioned Faith to in passing. Obviously, he had easily put two and two together. Brandon quickly showered, dressed and said his goodbyes.

He didn't realize how much he wanted to see Faith until he caught himself nearly sprinting across the hotel's parking lot to her room. *What am I doing?* He slowed to a walk, but the closer he got, the faster his heart raced with anticipation. He knocked and shoved his hands into his pockets to keep from hauling her into his arms as soon as she opened the door.

"May I help you?"

He masked his surprise at seeing the unfamiliar woman and took a hasty glance at the room number to make sure he was at the right one. He was six-four and towered over her by more than a foot. She had to be at least an inch or two shorter than Faith. The petite woman with honey-brown skin placed a hand on a curvy hip and lifted a brow. "I'm looking for Faith," he said.

"And you are?"

"Brandon."

A smile curved her lips and she slowly looked him up and down. "Well, well."

Not particularly caring for the scrutiny, he felt his irritation rising. "Is this her room?"

"Depends."

Before Brandon could form a reply, Faith appeared in the doorway.

Faith rolled her eyes at the woman. "Stop it, Kathi. Come on in, Brandon."

The woman chuckled and disappeared into a bedroom.

He followed Faith to the sofa and sat next to her. "How are you?" The swelling on her cheek seemed to be going down and the cuts on her face were healing, but she still favored her right arm.

"Getting better. Sorry about Kathi."

"No problem. Is she your sister?"

She laughed and shook her head. "No. Best friend and second mother," she added wryly. "She flew down for the weekend to help me out. What are you doing here?"

Brandon shrugged. "I was concerned about you and wanted to make sure you had everything you needed, but I see you're being well taken care of." He had a hard time understanding why he felt such disappointment. A strange reaction since he had never cared one way or another about a woman spending time with a friend, well, except for Lisa Wilson in the ninth grade, but that didn't count. He made a habit of steering clear of long-term relationships and usually had no problem moving on to the next woman. But there was still more he wanted to learn about Faith.

She placed her hand on his. "I know I said it before, but I can't tell you how much I appreciate all you've done to help me. If you hadn't been there that night... You are one of the nicest guys I've ever met. I wish..."

"You wish what?" he asked when she trailed off.

"Oh, nothing."

Brandon brought her hand to his lips and placed a kiss on the back. "It had to be something. What were you going to say?"

"I was just going to say I wish there were more people like you."

He had hoped she would say that, like him, she wished they had more time to explore whatever was happening between them. "Thank you." Not wanting to leave, but knowing he should, Brandon rose to his feet. "I don't want to intrude on your time with your friend. I just wanted to check on you."

Faith slowly came to her feet and trailed him to the door. "I'll see you later."

"Count on it." For a man who typically went out of his way to avoid anything more than a casual liaison, he seemed to be heading in the opposite direction.

Faith was glad Kathi had come to help, but would have liked to spend more time with Brandon.

"So that's Brandon," Kathi said.

She turned from the door, crossed the floor and reclaimed her seat on the sofa. "Yep."

"You were right. He's a gorgeous specimen of a man— tall, nicely built, and that face… *Mmm mmm mmm*."

"Is that why you were in the middle of grilling him like a suspect when I came to the door?"

Kathi placed her hand over her heart and feigned innocence. "Who, me?"

Faith skewered her friend with a look. "You really need to stop doing that. Brandon is a nice guy."

"What's going on between you two? You just met the man a couple of days ago and you're all defensive."

"I'm not being defensive."

Kathi studied Faith. "You like him, don't you?"

Faith shrugged. "What's not to like? Not only is he good-looking, but caring and thoughtful."

"What kind of job does he have?"

"He told me he works for a home safety company, but I don't know what he does exactly. And since I'm only going to be here a short time, he probably didn't think he needed to share all that." She remembered how quickly he had shifted the conversation when she had asked about it. "If we lived in the same city, I might like to see where this goes." She shared how he had held her hand while waiting for the ambulance, taken care of her belongings and visited her in the hospital. And when she was released, he'd driven her to the market and pharmacy, and then later brought her food. "I've never had a man I didn't know do such nice things for me without asking. Or one I did know," she added with a shake of her head. "I can't explain it, but he's different. A little bossy, but an all-around good guy." Her mind drifted to the sweet kiss he'd given her before leaving last night. She tried to push it aside and tell herself it meant nothing, but the memory of his firm lips moving sensuously over hers had had her tossing and turning all night and refused to stay buried.

Kathi laughed.

"What?"

"I thought you wanted to go shopping. If you sit here daydreaming about Brandon, we won't make it to the stores before closing."

Faith smiled. "Shut up. We have plenty of time."

"I don't know. That look on your face said we might be here awhile."

"Whatever, girl." She eased up from the sofa and went to retrieve her purse.

As they pulled out of the parking lot, Kathi said, "While you were talking to Brandon, I took the liberty of Googling nearby malls. There's a Westfield Mall in Culver City." She handed Faith her phone. "It's about five miles from here, straight down Sepulveda Boulevard."

Faith glanced down at the screen. "It says it should take about fifteen minutes." She needed a few shirts that buttoned down the front. She'd only brought a couple and trying to lift her arm to put on her pullover tees caused so much pain, she had been forced to sleep in the short hospital gown they had given her. She activated the turn-by-turn directions.

After a few minutes, Kathi asked, "So have you decided when you're going to call your father?"

Faith leaned her head against the seat and sighed heavily. "No. I was all for it when I first found out, but now I think I'm getting cold feet. But reading his letters makes me angry at my mother all over again. It breaks my heart that all he had were memories of me up to my second birthday. In some of those letters, he sounded so sad." Her emotions welled up again remembering reading one letter where he wrote about missing her so much sometimes that his heart hurt, but he wouldn't give up hope that he'd hold her in his arms again.

"Then maybe you should just go ahead and call him. It seems like he'll really be glad to see you."

"Maybe. I'm just really nervous about the whole thing."

Kathi found a parking spot in the crowded mall and cut the engine. "Do you have your father's address?"

"Yes, why?" She had saved the directions in her phone.

"I know you're not quite ready to meet him, but we could drive by his house after we leave just to see what kind of place he has."

She thought for a moment. She had never made it to his house the first time and she was curious about what it would look like. "Okay." They stopped first to check the store directory. "I don't want to spend a lot of money on clothes. I just need a few tops to get through the next few days. I should be okay by the end of the week."

Kathi pointed. "Here's a Target and an Old Navy. You should be able to find something in one of those places."

Faith did find some cute tops in both stores and at great prices. Afterward, they walked over to Subway. Use of her right hand was still limited, but she could manage a sandwich and some chips. Back in the car, she pulled up her father's address and gave Kathi directions.

Kathi groaned. "What is it with this city? It's the middle of the afternoon on a Saturday. Why is there traffic like it's Friday at rush hour?"

She laughed. "I have no idea. I've been here less than a week." It took ten minutes to go two miles and Faith considered telling Kathi to get off at the next exit and turn around so they could go back to the hotel. Finally, the traffic eased.

"This is a nice area," Kathi said after they exited the freeway.

It turned out that her father's house was only five minutes from the freeway and located in an established neighborhood with larger homes and manicured lawns. Faith pointed. "It's the one on the left with the black sedan in the driveway."

Kathi slowed to a stop and parked across the street, but left the engine running. "Nice house. Do you know if he's married or has other kids?"

"None of his letters mentioned a wife or children, but that doesn't mean anything." The one-story house didn't fit the picture of a bachelor. With the car in the driveway, she assumed he was home and silently wished he would step outside, just so she could see what he looked like. After another minute, she told Kathi, "We should probably leave so folks don't think we're up to something."

Kathi put the car in Drive and headed back the way they came.

Later, lying in bed, Faith thought about the recent changes in her life. Soon she would meet the man who had given her life. The man who, for twenty-eight years, had never stopped believing he'd find and reconnect with his daughter. But when she closed her eyes, it was face of the man who'd come to her rescue that she saw. The man who kissed her with a sweetness she had never experienced, the one who, despite her good judgment, she wanted to know more about.

Chapter 5

Monday afternoon, Faith and Kathi stood at the counter in the car rental office. "I'm so glad you came down." No matter what happened, she could always count on her best friend to be there. She smiled, remembering how Kathi had come over after Faith's last breakup. While watching a comedy movie, they had stuffed themselves with pepperoni and mushroom pizza, wine and popcorn. It had been just what Faith needed. And she had done the same for Kathi a time or two.

Kathi waved her off. "Girl, you know I had to make sure you were all right." She took the paperwork from the agent and penned her signature in all the designated areas. The woman handed Kathi her copy. "Thank you."

Faith got her rental, then drove Kathi to the airport. "Call me when you get home."

"I will. And you be careful with that arm. I'll be in and out for the rest of the week in a training class, but let me know what happens with your father…and Brandon. You wouldn't happen to know if he has any brothers, would you?"

She laughed. "No, I don't. And what about the guy you're supposed to be dating?"

"The key word is *dating*. Not married." A police officer outside the terminal blew his whistle. "Guess I'd better get going. Take care, sis."

"You, too. And thanks for being here."

Kathi climbed out of the car, grabbed her bag from the backseat, threw up a wave and disappeared inside the terminal.

Faith pulled away from the curb. With the construction, traffic and confusing signs, she got lost twice before finding her way out of the airport. She smiled thinking about Kathi's last statement. The woman was outrageous. But the question was a good one. She didn't know much about Brandon other than his first name, that he worked at a home safety company—a lot—and his family got together for dinner on some Sundays.

While driving, nervous flutters filled her belly. The last time she was behind the wheel hadn't ended well and she was very conscious of every car around her. Faith managed to make it back to the hotel without mishap and breathed a sigh of relief.

She spent the next hour working on a website, but kept getting distracted with thoughts of her father. Now that she had seen where he lived, she was even more curious about him. Her arm was healing nicely, so she needed to plan her visit. She saved her work and shut down the laptop.

She went to the kitchen and rummaged through the refrigerator for something to snack on. She settled for a container of peach yogurt. Though dressing and showering still gave her problems, she could finally get a spoon to her mouth without pain radiating all through her arm. She sat on the sofa, opened another one of her father's letters and read. She finished it and opened another. Her cell chimed, letting her know she had received a text message. It was Kathi.

Made it home.

She texted back: Glad to hear it.

She placed the cell on the table and unfolded the next letter. The words on the page brought tears to her eyes.

Hi, Faith. How's Daddy's baby girl? It's been five years since I've seen you and I know you're a big girl now. I miss you so much, sweetheart, and think about you all the time. I can't wait to see you again.
All my love,
Daddy

Faith was crying so hard she could barely see the words. She clutched the letter to her chest and let the tears fall. Once they finally stopped, she set the paper aside, stretched out on the sofa, closed her eyes and tried to bring her emotions under control. She had no idea how long she lay there before her cell rang. Instinctively, she reached for it with her right hand and winced with the pain. Coming to a sitting position, she picked it up with her left hand.

"Hello."

"Faith? Is everything okay?"

"Hey, Brandon. I'm fine." She cleared her throat and realized from all the crying she'd done, she probably sounded like she had a cold.

"Are you sure? You don't sound okay."

"I'm sure."

"Is your friend still there?"

"No. She left a few hours ago."

"Would it be okay if I came by after I leave work?"

"Of course." The words shot out of her mouth before she could stop them. *What am I doing? You agreed to one dinner, Faith*...one. *So why is it you have a sign that says "always open" whenever he calls?* She closed her eyes to shut out the annoying but logical voice inside her head. She knew she shouldn't be encouraging his visits, yet he made it so hard to resist. How often does a woman meet a guy like Brandon? Not often, so she planned to enjoy his company until she returned home.

"Faith!"

The sound of Brandon calling her name pulled her back into the conversation. "Huh? What? I'm sorry, what did you say?"

"Are you sure you're okay? I called your name three times."

"Fine, fine. My mind just drifted off for a minute. What time will you be here?"

"Around seven?"

"Great. I'll see you then." Faith ended the call and tapped the phone lightly against her forehead. "The man probably thinks you've lost your mind," she muttered. She stuffed the letter she'd read back into its envelope and placed it and the other one into the box, then took the box to her bedroom.

It dawned on her that Brandon was most likely coming from work and she didn't have anything to prepare for dinner. She had purchased some ready-to-eat meals, fruits and raw vegetables to compensate for her lack of function, but didn't think any of them would be suitable for entertaining. She took a quick peek at her watch. He wouldn't be there for another hour and she toyed with going out to buy something. But she nixed the idea because she didn't know the area well enough to go out searching. Instead of worrying about it, she sat at the table and powered up her laptop.

Faith was so engrossed in her work that the sharp knock

on the door startled her. When she opened the door, the sight of Brandon's smiling handsome face made her pulse skip.

"Hey."

"Hey, yourself." They stood there for several seconds just staring at each other. "Come in." She moved back so he could enter.

"Thanks." Instead of going over to the sofa like he usually did, Brandon closed the door behind him, tilted her chin and studied her for a long moment. "You've been crying. Why?"

How in the world hand he known? "It's nothing." Faith took a step and he placed a staying hand on her uninjured arm.

"Talk to me, Faith. Did something happen? Is it the pain? I can take you to the hospital." Evidently she didn't answer fast enough because he opened the door again. "Let's go."

"Brandon, wait. I'm not in pain."

He viewed her skeptically.

"Really." She closed the door and led him over to the sofa. "Yes, I was crying earlier when you called, but not from the pain. It's still stiff and sore, but nothing I can't handle. I can even move it a little. See?" She slowly lifted her arm midway and put it back down. "I told you I was in town for business."

Brandon nodded. "I remember."

"That's not exactly true. I recently found out that the father I believed dead is very much alive and has been looking for me for twenty-eight years. I came to LA to meet him. I was halfway to his house before I chickened out and was on my way back here the night of the accident."

"Wow. I mean…wow. I wasn't expecting that. But I don't understand how you thought he was dead, especially since he was looking for you all this time."

She gave him a sad smile. "You would if that's what your mother told you."

His stunned gaze met hers. "Your mother?" When she nodded, he asked, "Why would she do that?"

"He was in the military and suffered from PTSD. She said she was afraid he might hurt us, so she divorced him and packed up and left when I was two years old."

Brandon slid closer to Faith and draped an arm around her shoulder. "I'm sorry. I can't imagine growing up without my father."

"It's okay. My mother married my stepfather when I was eight, so I didn't grow up without a father. He's a wonderful man and I love him. Enough about me," she said, eager to change the subject. "Would you like something to drink? I have orange juice, tea and water. Sorry I don't have anything in the way of dinner to offer you. Me and the arm aren't quite ready for full-fledged cooking."

He chuckled. "It's no problem. We can go get something."

"Can we get it to go?"

"Sure."

Faith shut down her laptop. "I don't know what's around here, so you can choose."

"Whatever you want to do," he said in that black velvet voice.

"I'm… I'm going to change."

"Take your time."

She stood and backed away, unable to tear her gaze away. "I won't be long," she mumbled and retreated to the safety of her bedroom. This man did not play fair. How in the world was she supposed to resist him? "It's nothing serious, just some fun. All you have to do is keep your emotions out of it," she reminded herself as she slipped into a clean blouse.

* * *

Brandon followed Faith with his eyes and asked himself for the hundredth time why he couldn't stay away from her. It had only been two days since he'd seen her, but from the moment she opened the door and he saw her reddened eyes, he'd wanted to wrap her in his arms and make sure she never cried again. He thought about what she had told him. Even if his father had come back with the same issues, his mother would never have taken them away from their father. It had to be difficult for Faith, as well as her father, to know they'd missed out on so much time.

"I'm ready."

He rose to his feet. She had changed from the sweats to a sleeveless purple button-down top, black shorts and flat sandals. As they walked to his car, he said, "Oh, and this does *not* count as the dinner I promised you." He unlocked the doors by remote and held it open for her.

"Speaking of that, since this isn't really a date or anything, I'll pay for my own food. You've done so much already."

"I don't think so." He closed the door, got in on the other side and started the engine.

"Brandon—"

Brandon slanted her a sidelong glance. "Date or no date, you're not paying." He pulled out of the lot and onto the road. A few minutes into the ride, he looked over and saw her tightly set features. Was she mad because he wouldn't allow her to pay? When he started dating, his father had drilled into his and his brother's heads how they should treat a woman—always open doors, stand when she enters the room and never expect her to pay when you take her out. Brandon had taken those instructions to heart and didn't see that changing anytime soon. But he didn't want her angry with him, either. "Are you mad?"

Faith turned his way. "I haven't decided."

"What does that mean?"

"I'm not real fond of the whole bossy thing, but it's kind of flattering to be with a man who seems to be a throwback to the era where men didn't want women to pay for dates."

"You think I'm a throwback?"

"Maybe, but you're definitely bossy."

Brandon laughed. "Yeah, well, I already acknowledged that part. And after almost thirty-four years, I don't think it'll change."

She laughed. "Yep, you're pretty much set in your ways."

He started to ask her age, but gathered from what she had told him that she was thirty. "So, do you know what you want to eat?"

"No. What do you have a taste for?"

She'd asked the question so innocently, and what he wanted to answer was anything but. Yes, he had a taste for something, more like a craving, really. He wanted more of her sweet kisses, to trail his hands and lips over her smooth-as-silk skin and…

"Brandon?"

He cleared his throat and shifted in his seat. "Oh, nothing specific. There are several restaurants a few miles up the road, I'm sure we can find something."

Forty-five minutes later, they returned with meals from an Italian restaurant. He unloaded their pasta dishes at her small table while she got glasses from the cabinet for the lemonade. During the meal, Brandon tried his best not to think about kissing her, but watching her lips close around the fork and her tongue dart out to catch the sauce in the corner of her mouth had him so aroused he could barely eat. To distract himself, he said, "Tell me about your business."

Faith took a sip of her lemonade before speaking. "It actually started as a favor for a friend of mine who had a newly launched catering business. She wasn't happy with the person she had hired, didn't like the color scheme and the site wasn't user-friendly. This person stopped returning her calls and never made the requested changes, so she asked me to help her. I had so much fun. It just sort of snowballed from there. At the time, I worked as an assistant manager in a small software company."

"So you just quit?"

"Oh, no. I worked there another two years and did the website design program before striking out on my own. It's been just over a year and I've enjoyed every minute."

Brandon was impressed. She had done a lot in a short amount of time. "Do you plan to have a team of designers eventually?"

"I don't know. What I'd really like to do is offer classes to teens so they can gain entrepreneurship skills early on."

"That sounds like a great idea." He also thought it might be something to start at his company. *If it ever became his.*

"You told me you worked at a home safety company, but not exactly what you do. Although, with how bossy you are, I'd guess you're in some management position," Faith added with a smile.

He chuckled. "You're right, but I started at the bottom and worked my way up. We design and manufacture accessible equipment like shower rails and custom ramps."

"That's fantastic. How long have you been a manager?"

"Three years." Not wanting to talk about himself anymore, Brandon quickly shifted the conversation back to Faith. "Tell me more about this entrepreneurship idea you have."

She continued to share her plans, even after they had finished dinner. She spoke with such passion and enthusiasm he couldn't help but get caught up in her excitement. He watched the way her lips moved, fantasizing.

"I'm sorry. I've been going on and on. I didn't mean to bore you. I get a little excited when talking about my sites."

"You're not boring me."

"Are you sure? It looked like you were a million miles away. What were you thinking about?"

"Do you really want to know?" Brandon stood, rounded the table and gently pulled her to her feet. "This." He bent and covered her mouth in a heated kiss. The contact sent a sharp jolt to his groin. He slid an arm around her waist and pulled her closer, deepening the kiss. On the edge of losing control, he eased back.

"We need to slow down," Faith said, her breathing uneven. "I didn't come here for this. Only to meet my father."

"I know."

"It doesn't make sense to start something we know won't last."

"I agree, but it seems this *something* is beyond our control. How about a compromise?" he asked when she nodded. He placed kisses along her jaw and the curve of her neck.

"What kind?" she murmured.

"We see each other for the duration of your visit. Whatever we have ends when you leave." He wasn't looking for a commitment and he assumed she didn't want one, either.

"So, another couple of weeks or so."

"Yes."

She paused briefly, seemingly thinking over his offer. Then she nodded. "Okay."

He smiled and slanted his mouth over hers again. Two weeks wouldn't be nearly enough time to get her out of his system, but he'd take it.

Chapter 6

Tuesday, Brandon sat in his office making notes for the staff meeting later that morning. He thought more about having internships and learning modules for students and liked it. He jotted down all the areas of potential training and smiled. Faith had a brilliant idea. Faith. He leaned back in his chair and pondered their agreement. He had hoped for more than just two weeks with her and wanted her to stay awhile longer. Maybe if things worked out with her father, she'd reconsider.

"Uh-oh, I recognize that look," Justin said from the doorway.

"What look? I'm just thinking about a new proposal to present at the meeting." Brandon glanced over at the wall clock, stood and gathered his papers. "You coming?"

"After you." As they entered the conference room down the hall, Justin asked, "So, how's Faith?"

"She's good, healing."

"That's what I thought. Like I said, 'the look.'" And he walked away.

He didn't have any look. Justin didn't know what he was talking about. Brandon shook his head, got a cup of coffee and took a seat. The meeting started as usual with updates from each department.

"Mr. Gray, are you and Mr. Whitcomb still planning to step down at the end of the month?" someone asked from the other side of the room.

Brandon's jaw tightened.

Brandon's father and uncle shared a look before his father spoke. "Brandon's transition to CEO will be delayed for another few weeks. There are a couple of loose ends Thad and I need to tie up first, then we will proceed as planned."

Siobhan asked, "Is it something we can help with?"

"I appreciate the offer, but we have it under control. Rest assured this is nothing that will affect the running of the company in any way."

She gave Brandon a look that said "I tried."

There were a few more updates, and then Brandon gave his. He also presented the idea of having interns and conducting entrepreneur workshops for teens, which was well received. At the end of the meeting, he left the room without talking to anyone, still annoyed by whatever was delaying his takeover as CEO.

After lunch, Siobhan knocked and entered. "You okay?"

"Fine."

She sat across from him. "I went to Daddy's office and tried to get some information, but he is seriously close-mouthed on this. I'm even more curious as to what's going on. He's never been like this when it comes to business."

"Exactly. Which is why I'm worried." Had this been something pertaining to family business, Brandon wouldn't have batted an eye because their parents had kept details about certain things from them until the right time.

"Well, he did reiterate that this doesn't affect you getting the job, just in case someone thinks they have a shot. So, that should make you feel better."

"Maybe. But something just *feels* off about this. I know what Dad said, but somehow, I know this is going to have an impact on me and how I do my job."

Siobhan shrugged. "Mom might know something. You can always ask her at dinner on Sunday."

He let out impatient sigh. "Yeah, right. You know good and well Mom isn't going to betray any secrets."

"True." She waved a hand. "Enough about that. I heard you were still visiting that woman from the accident. Are you two getting serious?"

Brandon planned to punch Justin on sight. "No. She's just visiting LA and will only be here for a couple of weeks."

"Since she doesn't know anyone here, you should bring her to the family dinner on Sunday."

His eyes widened. "Oh, hell no!"

"Goodness, Brandon," she said with a chuckle. "No need to bite my head off. It was just a suggestion." She stood and walked to the door. "See you later."

Brandon shook his head. No way would he take Faith to that dinner. That would be tantamount to making a statement. And he wasn't. They were just enjoying each other until she left for Portland. No ties. No commitments. Just the way he liked it.

Tuesday evening, Faith sat on bed in her hotel room flipping through the channels, but didn't find anything that remotely interested her. As she reached for the book on her nightstand, her cell rang. "Hi, Daddy," she said when she picked up.

"How are you feeling, sweet baby girl?"

Faith smiled at the name her stepfather always called her. "I'm doing okay. My face and head don't hurt anymore, but my arm is still sore, especially when I try to lift it over my head." She cradled the phone against her ear and adjusted the blanket across her legs with her left hand.

"Maybe you should come home for a while…until you're all healed up. I'm worried about you being there all alone with no one to help you."

She knew he would say that, which was why she hadn't called since the accident. "Daddy, I'm fine. The worst of it is over and Kathi was here over the weekend. I'll be home soon."

He paused. "Your mother is really worried about you, Faith. You two need to work this out."

"It takes two," she mumbled. "How is she?"

He chuckled. "Still mad. But then you're both stubborn. I love you both and I can see how this is tearing you apart. I'm telling you the same thing I told her—you two need to talk."

Faith released a deep sigh. "I'll call her later in the week."

"Thanks, baby. Have you contacted your father yet?"

"No," she said softly. "With the accident and all, I didn't want to just drop that on him."

"I understand. Well, I won't hold you. I love you very much. Always remember that."

"I love you too, Daddy." She disconnected and groaned. Faith and her mother were more alike than she cared to admit. Both had a stubborn streak that probably accounted for most of their disagreements. Growing up, her dad had been the peacemaker and neither she nor her mother could stay angry for long periods of time. He always found a way to make them smile.

Putting her mother out of her mind for now, Faith

shifted her thoughts to her birth father. All the bravado she had felt when she first came to LA had faded and nervousness had taken its place. She'd been in town a week and couldn't afford to stay indefinitely, so she needed to put on her big girl panties and make that drive.

It took her until the end of the week to decide. Saturday midday, she followed the directions back to her father's house. The black sedan was parked in the same spot. Faith sat in the car for a few minutes to gather her courage. She picked up the small book on the seat, got out and started up the walkway. The lawn looked freshly mowed and an array of colorful flowers lined the front of the house. She rang the bell and nervously wrung her hands while waiting. She heard the lock turn and her heart started to pound.

The door opened and she gasped softly. Aside from the sprinkling of gray in his close-cropped hair and neatly barbered goatee, he looked as if he hadn't aged a day in almost three decades. He stood close to six feet, was still trim and his dark handsome face was virtually unlined. Her gaze drifted to the crutches under his arm and down to see that his left leg had been amputated at the knee.

A smile creased his face. "Hello. May I help you?"

Faith had no idea how to introduce herself. She fidgeted for a moment, opened and closed her mouth, searching for the right words. "I'm Faith." His brows knit and confusion lined his face. Then she saw the moment he realized who she was.

"Faith?" he whispered. "*My* Faith?"

She nodded.

Tears filled his eyes and he grabbed her in a crushing hug. "Thank God. My baby girl," he said over and over. He held her as if he never wanted to let go and deep, heart-wrenching sobs erupted from his throat.

She felt every inch of his pain and couldn't stop her own tears. They stood in the doorway and cried out twenty-eight years of separation. At length, they quieted, but he didn't release her. Finally, he leaned back. "I didn't ever think I'd find you," he said emotionally, swiping at the tears on his cheeks. "Forgive me for keeping you standing on the porch. Please, come in." He maneuvered on his crutches so she could enter.

Faith stepped into an immaculate and elegantly furnished living room. Two landscape paintings hung on the walls, but no family pictures. Her curiosity heightened. Had he ever remarried or had other children?

"We can talk in the family room. Can I get you something to drink? Are you hungry?" he asked as he led her down a short hall and through the kitchen to another room.

"No, thank you." The family room held a large bookcase, fireplace, a brown, fabric-covered sectional with recliners and another oversize recliner. She instinctively knew he spent much of his time here. A pair of glasses sat atop a book on an end table next to the chair and the sports news was muted on a large-screened TV. He gestured her to sit and she perched on the edge of the sofa, gripping the book in her hands tightly, unsure about what to say or do.

Thad set the crutches aside and lowered himself into the recliner. For a long moment, he just stared at her. He shook his head. "I can't believe you're here. I prayed for so long. You were a beautiful baby and you've grown into an even more beautiful woman."

Heat stung her cheeks. "Thank you. I… I don't know what to call you."

He smiled softly. "How about Thad for now?"

"Okay." She agreed, but truthfully, she was a little uncomfortable calling him by his first name. She had been raised to respect her elders and to never call them by their first names, unless she preceded it with mister, miss, aunt or uncle.

"Tell me a little bit about you. What do you do?"

"I own my own website design business."

"Wow. That's fantastic. My baby girl is her own boss. How about that?" he said, seemingly more to himself.

Faith smiled. "It's only been a year since I had enough steady work to quit my day job. I worked as an assistant manager in a software company, so the learning curve wasn't too tough."

Thad chuckled. "What made you decide to switch careers?"

She shared with him the same story she told Brandon. "I've done sites for two musical artists, a couple of medical offices and my newest one is a construction company."

"I always knew you would do well. When you were small, whenever we tried to help you do something, you'd snatch away, say, 'I do, I do' and take off running." He chuckled, then sobered. "I missed so much."

She met his eyes. "We both did." Silence crept between them. "I brought some pictures of me growing up. I thought it might…" His eyes lit up and he came to sit next to her. She handed him the album and watched as he ran his hand over the cover photo of her taken at age four at a park.

"So beautiful." He opened it and, for the next while, Faith explained each picture. She had chosen ones she hoped would give him a good representation of her formative years—walking into her first day of kindergarten, standing next to her winning science fair board in fifth grade, holding her second place spelling bee ribbon in eighth grade and running track her junior and senior years. She had also included some candid shots and her high school and college graduation photos.

At the end, he reached for her hand. "Thank you for sharing these." He handed the book to her.

Faith gave his hand a gentle squeeze. "It's yours to keep. I know it doesn't make up for all the time you missed, but

I hope it fills in a few of the pieces." She felt her emotions rising again and blinked back the moisture in her eyes.

Thad nodded and clutched the book to his chest.

Her cell rang and she jumped slightly. "Excuse me." She fished it out of her purse and saw Brandon's name on the display. "Hello."

"Hey, beautiful. What are you up to?"

"I'm visiting my…" She cut a quick look at Thad. "My father. Can I call you back?"

"Of course. I hope everything goes well for you."

"Thank you." She ended the call and dropped the phone in her purse. "Sorry about that."

He laughed. "I'd be worried if it didn't ring at least once. So, is there a special guy in your life?"

An image of Brandon flashed in her mind and she quickly dismissed it. "No," she answered with a chuckle. "I've never been married and I don't have any children." She debated on whether to ask him the same questions. "What about you?"

Thad shook his head. "No. I never remarried and you're my one and only. Did Francis ever remarry?"

"Yes, when I was eight, but no other children." Seeing the sadness reflected in his face, she felt even worse. She'd had her mother and stepfather, but he'd had no one to share his life. Had he been one of those men who could only love once? Or had something else happened? She didn't know him well enough to pry, so set the questions aside.

He brightened. "My best friend and his wife have five children and they've adopted me as an uncle. I broke down and bought this house because when their three boys spent the night, they almost got me evicted from my condo with all the noise." He smiled. "They were running and sliding on the wood floors, turning flips and hitting the walls. My neighbors were not happy."

Laughter bubbled up and spilled from Faith's lips. "How old were they?"

"Nine, seven and four. But I love those boys and their sisters."

She could hear the affection in his voice. A part of her was envious of the time they had spent with her father. Time that should have been hers. But another part of her was glad he hadn't spent all those years alone. Faith glanced down at her watch. She had been there for three hours. "Do you still see them?"

"Yes. All the time."

She wondered if she'd ever get a chance to meet them. "Well, I know you probably have lots of things to do and I don't want to take up all your time."

"Faith, I don't have anything planned that tops seeing you." Thad seemed to weigh his next words. "How long are you going to be here?"

"A week or two."

"Oh." She could hear the disappointment in his voice. "Any chance of you staying longer? I just found you again and I…" He trailed off.

Faith totally understood. "I'll try. And even if I can't, I will come back."

"That's all I can ask for. Where are you staying?"

She gave him the name of the hotel, her room number and her cell phone number.

"Do you think we can go to dinner sometime next week?"

"I'd like that very much." She was glad he had suggested they have dinner at a later date because she needed a few days to process everything. Faith stood.

Thad reached for his crutches and followed suit.

They walked to the front door. She turned to face him. "I'm really glad I came."

"So am I." He gathered her in his embrace once again and moved back. "I'll call you so we can set up a time."

"Okay." She strolled to her car and got in. She glanced toward the house and saw him waving. She waved back and pulled off.

Her mind went back to his request for her to stay longer. They had so much to catch up on that two weeks wouldn't even scratch the surface. But she had to pay rent on her town house and the hotel wasn't cheap. She didn't want to dip into her savings. However, extending her time would give her more time to learn about his life. And more time with Brandon.

Chapter 7

Brandon leaned against the wall of his parents' game room and waited for Khalil to take his turn at the pool table.

"So, did you ask Mom about what's going on?" Khalil walked around the table, lined up his shot and sent the ball sailing into a corner pocket.

"No. You know she's not going to say anything Dad said not to tell. And I know he's told her."

"True. At least they're consistent. Nothing's changed in thirty-seven years."

Brandon laughed. Their parents had been together for almost four decades and made no secret that they were each other's confidante.

"I asked Dad about it and he shut me down cold. Vonnie said he did the same thing to her."

"Yeah." The announcement had bugged him all week, since the time his father had made it during the staff meeting. His grip tightened on the stick and he hit the ball so hard three of them went into pockets, including one of his brother's. He cursed under his breath.

Khalil chuckled. "Thanks, bro."

Brandon ignored him. Not wanting to spoil his Sunday family dinner, he changed the subject. "I saw part of the gym blocked off when I was there on Thursday. You're not wasting any time."

"They've started installing the new floor. I really like how it feels. It's almost better than the actual mats."

"You could use it for the whole gym."

"I thought about it, but the cost would be astronomical with all the square footage."

"Well, Mr. Big Bucks, you can afford it."

"Maybe, but there's no sense in throwing away my money. I'd like to remain *Mr. Big Bucks*," he added wryly. Khalil had started modeling professionally at sixteen and spent a decade gracing the covers of several magazines. He had been the face of several products, an international spokesperson for fitness and even had cameo appearances in two movies.

As they finished the game, Malcolm and his two brothers-in-law joined them. Brandon and Khalil relinquished the table to Omar and Malcolm.

Midway through their game, Morgan came in to let them know dinner was ready. Brandon always looked forward to these dinners because his mama could cook. It was the one thing he missed the most after moving out. The fragrant smells had hit his nose the moment he arrived and he couldn't wait to dive in.

His father blessed the food and Brandon filled his plate with fried chicken, slices of prime rib, macaroni and cheese, roasted asparagus, sautéed corn and homemade rolls. He groaned with the first bite of his chicken. "Mom, *nobody* makes chicken like yours."

A chorus of agreements met his statement.

His father picked up his glass of iced of tea. "I'd like to propose a toast to Malcolm and Omar. May you both be blessed this football season and may the Cobras bring home the championship trophy again."

They all raised their glasses. This would most likely be their last family dinner until the end of the season, unless his mother tried to schedule one before the end of July or during their bye week.

Conversation flowed around the table as they ate.

"Brandon, are you still seeing that woman you helped from the accident?" Justin asked casually, not looking up from his plate.

"Is this the friend you took off early for a couple of weeks back?" his father asked.

His mother's eyes lit up. "Does this mean she's a potential daughter-in-law?"

Brandon froze. Every eye around the table turned his way. He glared at Justin. "It's not like that, Mom. And yes, Dad, she's the one. She had just arrived in town for business the day before the accident. She doesn't know anyone here, so I was just being the gentleman you raised me to be." Okay, so that wasn't entirely the truth. The whole "just being friendly" thing had gone by the wayside the first time he tasted her lips.

"I don't know about this taking off work early. Wouldn't want anything to *distract* you from the job."

He focused his gaze on Morgan.

"Exactly," Siobhan chimed in. "You really need to make sure you're available in case something comes up."

Both of his sisters were throwing his words back in his face. He guessed he deserved it, but at the time, he thought he had been right.

Justin chuckled.

Brandon eyes him across the table, sorely tempted to knock that smug look off Justin's face. "Look—"

Siobhan muttered something that sounded like, "Oh, God," slapped a hand over her mouth and bolted from the room. Justin tossed down his napkin and rushed out behind her.

The family looked on with concern. A few tense minutes later, they returned.

His father stood. "What's going on?"

Siobhan and Justin shared a smile and Siobhan said, "Well, this isn't exactly how I planned to tell it, but we're having a baby."

His mother jumped up and ran around the table. "Thank You, Lord! A grandbaby!" She engulfed the expectant parents in a warm hug. "I'm so happy for you both."

Brandon rose to his feet. "This calls for another toast." Everyone stood and raised their glasses. "To Justin and Vonnie. Wishing you an abundance of God's blessing as you begin this new journey. Congratulations."

A round of congrats, hear, hears, and amens sounded in the room.

"What a wonderful addition to our family," his mother said. "Hopefully, I'll have a new daughter soon, too."

Brandon groaned inwardly. He heard snickers from his brothers and turned a blazing look their way. He managed to get through the rest of dinner without any more comments.

After everyone had recuperated from the lavish meal, dessert was served. Today's offering was another of Brandon's favorites—brownies loaded with chocolate chips, topped with his father's homemade ice cream. He would definitely have to add an additional visit to the gym this week to offset all the calories he'd consumed.

Malcolm entered and sat in the chair next to Brandon. "So, big brother's got a new woman, huh?"

"No, I do not. I told you she's just here for business and

I helped her out." He didn't share what type of business because he didn't feel it was necessary.

"Whatever. Better you than me, though."

"I second that," Khalil said, joining them. "I need a little variety in my life and I like having my own space." He ate a bite of his sundae. "What does she look like?"

Brandon hesitated. His brother loved beautiful women and had no qualms about staking a temporary claim on one, especially if Brandon said he wasn't interested. Women had been falling at Khalil's feet since grade school and Brandon didn't want Faith to be one of them.

Malcolm angled his head and gestured with his spoon. "You're taking a long time to answer. Is she that ugly?"

"She's not ugly at all."

Malcolm and Khalil grinned.

He divided his gaze between his brothers. "What?"

Khalil leaned forward. "I think big brother is trying to keep her a secret because he knows she'll like me better."

"Or me," Malcolm said. "He is getting up there in age."

"Would you two knock it off?" Growing up, whenever Brandon showed interest in a girl, the two of them would tease him mercilessly.

They burst out laughing.

Brandon shook his head and went out to the backyard deck to finish his dessert. Against his better judgment, he called Faith. They hadn't talked after her visit to her father and he wanted to know how things went. At least that was what he told himself. A more honest assessment centered on him just wanting to hear her voice. He had never felt this compelling need to call a woman. For some reason, he couldn't dismiss her as easily as with other women.

"Hey, Brandon," Faith said when she picked up the phone.

"Hi, baby."

"Sorry I didn't call you back yesterday. I just needed a moment."

"That's okay." Coming face-to-face with a man she believed to have been dead must have been emotionally draining, he suspected. "How did it go?"

"Surprisingly well. We talked for a long time and made plans for dinner this coming week."

"I'm sure that's a load off your mind."

"It definitely was. He seems to be a genuinely nice man and I'm sorry I didn't get a chance to know him."

They both fell silent. It had to be hard for both Faith and her father to know they'd lost so much time. "Since the visit went well, do you think you might be staying in LA longer?"

"He asked and I told him I'd consider it."

Brandon didn't know why her response made him so happy. He heard laughter and turned to see Siobhan and Justin in the far corner of the yard. He observed their smiles, the look of adoration on Justin's face as he placed a gentle hand on Siobhan's stomach and the tender kiss he placed on her lips. They were totally into each other. Was that—?

"Brandon?"

Faith's voice broke into his thoughts. "I'm sorry. What did you say?"

"I just asked if you had a busy week ahead."

He let out a short bark of laughter. "Every week is a busy one, but I don't mind." His gaze strayed back to the yard and a strange sensation stirred in his belly. "Ah, Faith, can I call you later? I'm at my parents' house right now. I just wanted to see if everything went okay yesterday."

"Of course. Enjoy yourself."

"I'll talk to you soon." He disconnected and scrubbed a hand down his face. He had a problem.

* * *

Faith was enjoying dinner with Thad Wednesday evening. He had chosen Harold & Belle's, a restaurant he'd said was like having a bit of New Orleans in Los Angeles. The space was open and done in varying shades of brown and tan and she liked the warm and cozy atmosphere. Thad had insisted on picking her up when she said she would meet him there and his response had been similar to Brandon's when she'd offered to pay for her meal. Both were gentlemen.

"You told me about your business last time. Where do you see yourself five to ten years from now?" Thad asked.

She shared her dream of starting a youth entrepreneurship program. "But that won't be for a while." She had told him a lot about herself and understood his need to learn as much as possible, but she was curious about his life, as well. "Are you still working or have you retired?"

Thad set his fork on the plate. "I work as a VP in a home safety company. We manufacture everything from bath rails and specialized mattresses to in-home alert systems."

Vice president. He had obviously done well for himself after serving in the armed forces. "How did you get into that field?"

"My buddy Nolan and I were in the army together and started the company when we got out after the Gulf War—he voluntarily and me…for medical reasons."

She saw the pain reflected in his face and regretted asking the question. "I'm sorry. I didn't mean to—"

Thad waved her off. "It's been over twenty-five years. And you have a right to know. I lost my leg in a Scud missile attack on the barracks. I was one of the lucky ones." His voice became distant. "We lost twenty-eight soldiers and close to a hundred more were injured. It was the worst thing I've ever seen. I had a prosthesis, but it was bothering me, so I had to be fitted for a new one. Hopefully, it won't be too long before it gets here."

Faith couldn't even begin to imagine the horrors he must have seen. Now she understood why he hadn't included any more photos with the letter after his discharge. "I'm very glad that you were one of the lucky ones."

"So am I. Even more so now." They continued eating in silence for a few minutes. Then he asked, "What did your mother tell you about us?"

She pushed the food around on her plate. She knew the question would eventually come up, but still she wasn't prepared and didn't want to hurt him any more than he'd been already. "She didn't say much."

"Faith?"

She blew out a long breath and met his eyes. "She told me you died serving in the military when I was two."

Thad dropped his head. "I guess after she sent the divorce papers, I was dead to her. I know she was uncomfortable about the flashbacks and dreams the first time I had a nightmare. I'm just sorry you got caught in the middle."

That was it? She expected him to say more. "You aren't angry?"

"I was for a long time. Angry at her, the army…God. But, after a while and some much-needed counseling, I came to understand that she'd done what she thought best at the time." He patted her hand. "And I know you're probably very angry with her, sweetheart, but you've got to let go of that anger. Otherwise, it will eat you alive. Believe me, I know. We can only go forward from here."

Faith had already determined that Thaddeus Whitcomb was a good man, but her admiration and respect for him shot up the charts. "I'm working on it." When he lifted a brow, she added, "It's the best I can do for now."

Thad chuckled. "Okay, I'll go with that. If you ever want to talk about it, or anything else, I'll be here. Always."

"I know." She gave him a small smile and finished her meal.

Later, after he'd dropped her off, Thad's words still played over in her mind. She was trying hard to let go of the irritation and resentment toward her mother. Her heart ached for Thad. Had he gone through all of that pain alone?

She heard a low buzzing sound and it took a moment to realize it was her cell phone. She dug it out of her purse and quickly answered before it could go to voice mail.

"Hey, beautiful lady," Brandon said.

Her pulse skipped with the endearment flowing from his low, sexy voice. "What's up, Brandon?"

"I'm calling to see if you're up for that dinner I owe you."

Faith smiled. The function in her right arm had almost returned to normal. "I most certainly am."

"Good. Then I'll pick you up tomorrow around six."

"I'm looking forward to it."

"Me, too. Good night, Faith."

"Good night." *I'm going to miss him when I go home.* She was still holding the phone when it rang again.

"Hey, girl," Faith said to Kathi.

"You know I'm calling for an update on your dad *and* Brandon. And don't leave out any details."

She laughed and caught her friend up on everything that had happened during her visit with Thad and their dinner. "He's a really nice man. I wonder how my life would've been if he and Mom hadn't divorced. And he's not even mad at her anymore. He said we have to move forward."

"Wow. He does have a point, though. So what are you going to do about your mom? Have you talked to her?"

"No," she said with a sigh. "I've talked to my dad and he basically said the same thing as Thad—that we need to work it out."

"Well, I'm glad everything is going well with Thad,

and I hope you and your mom can get past this. So, what's going on with you and that scrumptious male specimen who came to your door?"

Faith chuckled. "You are a mess. He's pretty nice, too. We've talked a few times and we've done takeout. When I was in the hospital, Brandon promised to take me out to dinner, so we're doing that tomorrow."

Kathi's heavy sigh came through the line. "Forget about that stuff. I want to know the juicy parts, like if he's kissed you yet."

She knew what her friend wanted to know, but didn't really want to share those details. "Yes, he kissed me."

"Kissed you how? Are we talking a little peck-on-the-cheek kiss or a melt-your-panties kiss?"

Leave it to Kathi to get right to the heart of the matter. "It was closer to the melt-your-panties side." Though the kiss was hot, she still sensed him holding back.

"Yeah, with a face and body like that, I wouldn't expect anything less. This could be the start of something good between you two."

"I don't think so."

"California is only one state away and you guys could easily have a relationship."

"Kathi, I have enough trouble maintaining relationships as it is. No way am I going to add distance to the equation. Besides, I don't think he's looking for anything serious, especially since he knows I'm leaving soon." Brandon hadn't said anything about a relationship and she wasn't going to assume he wanted anything other than their dinner date or to see each other until she left as agreed.

"Speaking of that, when are you coming home?"

"I had already planned to be back this weekend. Thad asked me to stay longer and I'm still deciding when to come back. Can you pick me up on Sunday afternoon?"

"Sure. Text me your flight info. Hey, I know where's

he's coming from. He just got you back after twenty-eight years. I'd want you to stay longer, too. You can do your job anywhere, so why not hang out another couple of weeks?"

"This hotel isn't cheap, even though I'm getting a good weekly rate. I still have the rent on my town house, so in a sense, I have two payments. I'll have to start dipping into my savings soon."

"You know I'll help you out, just like you did for me." When Kathi had started her job four years ago, there was a glitch in the company's system and she hadn't been able to get her paycheck for an additional two weeks. Faith had loaned her money to pay her rent.

"I know and I appreciate the offer. We can talk about it when I come home."

"All right. Ah…by the way, you know staying means more time with Brandon, too. I bet you've already thought about that," Kathi said with a giggle. "And what woman wouldn't want more time with him?"

Faith laughed. What woman, indeed? "I'm hanging up, crazy woman." She didn't want her friend to know that she had not only thought about it, but knew it would factor heavily into her decision.

Chapter 8

In anticipation of her date with Brandon, Faith got up the next morning and went back to the same mall she and Kathi had gone to before to find an outfit. She hadn't anticipated needing evening wear. Brandon would most likely be coming from work and wearing another pair of expensively tailored slacks and dress shirt, so she needed something a little dressier than the clothing she'd brought on the trip. It took the better part of the morning to find and settle on a pale blue sleeveless sheath and a pair of three-inch heeled black sandals with a matching purse. She only wished there had been time to have her hair washed and styled.

When she opened the door to Brandon that evening, the appreciative gleam in his eyes let her know that he approved of her choice, as well.

Brandon's gaze made a slow tour down her body, then back up again. "You look absolutely beautiful."

"Thank you." She moved back so he could enter. He bent and placed a soft kiss on her lips and his nearness sent a flurry of sensations down her spine. "I just need to get my purse."

He nodded, still staring at her. His gaze followed her every move and when she came back, he gestured her toward the door.

Brandon escorted her out to his car and helped her in. After getting in and pulling out of the lot and onto the road, he said, "I thought we'd go to Chart House in Marina Del Rey. They serve seafood, steaks, chicken…"

"Sounds good and I'm starving." Faith hadn't eaten a big lunch in anticipation of dinner. She made herself comfortable for the ride and watched the passing scenery. With the traffic the drive took nearly forty minutes.

The hostess seated them in the outside area of the upscale waterfront restaurant and, at Brandon's request, Faith shared more about her visit with her father while they dined on peach-bourbon-glazed scallops and shrimp, and prime rib.

"He must have been surprised and happy to see you."

"He was." She thought about their emotional reunion.

Brandon reached for her hand and pointed toward the water.

They sat in silence, watching as the sun set in a blaze of orange and reds across the sky. "It's amazing." And so was he. How many men would be content to sit and enjoy the simple pleasure of a sunset?

"I agree." Their eyes met. "Stunning."

The intensity of his stare told her he meant more than the sunset. She gently withdrew her hand and resumed eating.

When they finished, he settled the bill and asked, "Would you like to take a walk?"

"I'd love to." Because they were close to the water, the temperatures had dipped and a slight breeze had kicked up.

He entwined their fingers and they strolled off. He

stopped a ways down the path and faced her. For a moment, he said nothing, seemingly struggling with what he wanted to say.

"What is it?"

"I can show you better than I can tell you," Brandon whispered and lowered his head.

Faith clung to his muscular shoulders as he plundered her mouth. He eased her closer and she felt every inch of his hard frame pressed against her. She moaned softly.

At length, he lifted his head. Still gifting her with fleeting kisses along her jaw and the shell of her ear, he murmured, "We should probably head out before we really give these folks a show." But he didn't stop.

"Brandon." His name came out on a breathless whisper.

"Yeah, baby. I know."

Hearing him call her "baby" made her heart skip a beat. She briefly fantasized about how it would be if she were his. This had been one of the most romantic evenings she had ever experienced. When it came time for her to return home, she would have this night with Brandon as one of her treasured memories.

He kissed her once more, took her hand and retraced their steps to the car.

Faith's body hummed with desire. She clasped her hand in her lap, squeezed her thighs together and drew in several calming breaths. Goodness, he had only kissed her. What would happen if he did more? She shivered.

"Cold?"

"No. I'm fine."

"Is there any type of music you'd like to listen to? I should have asked on the drive here."

"What you're playing is nice." A midtempo soul groove flowed through the speakers. There was still a fair amount of traffic on the streets. "I don't know how you deal with traffic all the time. It's after eight o'clock."

Brandon laughed. "It's gotten really bad in the last decade or so, but I've lived here my whole life, so…" He shrugged.

Faith shook her head. "Our traffic is bad, but nothing like this."

He slanted her an amused glance. "Actually, this isn't bad. We're moving steadily, made most of the lights so far and I haven't gone below thirty miles per hour."

She burst out laughing. "Wow. Okay. I guess I'd better be quiet before I jinx us."

They got caught at the very next light and Brandon turned her way. "See, you messed up my groove."

She tried to look contrite, but couldn't stop laughing. She was still chuckling when they arrived back at the hotel.

Brandon placed his arm around her shoulder as they walked across the lot. "I can't believe you're still laughing."

"I can't help it, and you should've seen your face." After her statement, they'd missed most of the remaining lights and he barely cracked a smile. "Are you always so serious?" She unlocked the door.

"Sometimes, but I smile when it's called for," he said, following her in and closing the door.

Faith elbowed him playfully. "You can smile a little more. Go ahead."

He smiled.

"Aw, come on. You can do better than that. It won't hurt." She placed a hand on his arm. "I promise."

Brandon threw his head back and laughed.

The rich, warm sound filled the room. His eyes sparkled and her belly flipped. He had a beautiful laugh.

"Come here." He gathered her in his embrace. "You're something else, you know that?"

"I don't know what you mean," she teased.

His smile faded and he traced a finger down her cheek. "I want to kiss you again, Faith."

Faith nodded her consent and was, once again, swept away. His hands roamed down her back and settled on her hips briefly before moving around to cup her buttocks. She moaned, slid her arms around his neck and drew him closer. He gripped her tighter and pulled her flush against his erection, turning her legs to jelly. She felt the slide of the zipper on her dress, then the warmth of his strong hands on her bare back. He pushed the dress off her shoulders and charted a path of butterfly kisses along the column of her neck and over her shoulder. She knew she should stop him, but the sensations whipping through her had her in such a haze that she could do nothing but stand there and feel.

He gently turned her around and trailed his tongue down the center of her spine while his hands caressed her breasts. Faith's breaths came in short gasps and her knees buckled. "Brandon," she pleaded.

"I can't stop touching you and kissing you." Brandon spun her around and captured her mouth again in a scorching kiss. "If you're not ready for what I want to give you, tell me now." He nipped her bottom lip. "Say something, baby."

Her body wanted him so bad, but her head just wasn't ready. She'd barely known him three weeks. Her inner self warred for a few hot seconds. "We need to slow down," she finally managed. "I don't think I'm ready yet."

Brandon lifted his head and nodded. He redid her clothes and wrapped his arms around her. "Whenever you're ready, just let me know. If you just want to talk, tell me. You want me to massage your back, to touch you like this." His hand skimmed her thigh. "Or kiss you," he continued passionately, "call me. You won't have to beg and I won't make you wait. All you need to do is ask." He reclaimed her mouth in a long, drugging kiss. Then he was gone.

Faith collapsed into the nearest chair. "Lord, what a man!"

* * *

Brandon left Faith and drove straight to the gym. His body was so aroused and wound up he would never sleep tonight if he didn't work off the sexual tension. A cold shower wasn't going to cut it. After forgetting his gear a few weeks back, he'd started keeping a bag in his trunk and it would save a trip home first.

At this late hour, he prayed Khalil had already gone home. If he saw Brandon, he would immediately know what was up. And after all the teasing Sunday, that was the last thing Brandon needed. He had enough problems. The emotionally charged words he spoke to Faith had come from a place deep inside him he didn't even know existed. He had never uttered anything like that to another woman, and in fact made a practice to steer clear of any sentiments that could be misconstrued as him wanting anything beyond the moment. Maybe it had to do with the intimate atmosphere at the restaurant. *Yeah, that's it.* Shaking it off, he chalked it up to a strong physical desire. As soon as they slept together, he'd be back to normal.

He changed clothes and headed for the treadmill, scanning the room and upstairs offices for his brother. All the office lights were off. Relaxing, he started the machine.

Five minutes into his run, Brandon's mind went back to Faith—the smooth texture of her dark brown skin, the alluring swell of her breasts above the black lace bra and the intoxicating taste of her lips. If she hadn't stopped him when she did, he would not have left until he knew every inch of her sexy body. Intimately. So lost in thought, he didn't realize he'd slowed down. Brandon stumbled and almost fell off the machine. He gripped the bar and cursed. Regaining his balance, he focused on finishing the thirty-minute cycle.

Afterward, he used a towel to wipe his face and crossed the room to do his leg workout. His legs were on fire by the time he completed the exercises. He rested for two minutes and moved over to the bench press. He had just finished the second set when a shadow fell over him.

"Thinking about a woman while trying to run at full speed on the treadmill can get you killed."

He tilted his head forward and met Khalil's smiling face. "What the hell are you still doing here?"

Khalil folded his arms, his grin still in place. "This is *my* gym. I don't have to justify why I'm here. You, on the other hand… Let me guess, you're ready to take things to the next level and she's not, leaving you frustrated and horny as hell."

Brandon snatched the bar off the rack and did his next set. He replaced the bar. "Don't you have somebody to train or somewhere to be?"

"That bad, huh?" He chuckled. "This isn't the first time you've come in to work off your frustrations, but I sense something else going on with you."

His brother had always been good at reading Brandon, as well as all their siblings. And he hated it. "I don't need a damn psych evaluation, I just need to finish my workout in peace." Khalil stood at the end of the bench. "Do you mind?"

Khalil stepped to the left. "If she's not ready, maybe you should move on. Isn't that what you typically do?"

Brandon had planned to finish his upper body, but the urge to punch Khalil was so strong, he opted for the heavy bag instead. "If you say one more word, I'm gonna risk Mama's wrath and knock the hell out of you." The last time they'd gotten into a brawl, he had been twenty-five and Khalil, twenty-three. He couldn't remember why they were fighting, but during the scuffle had broken two of their parents' deck chairs and ruined their mother's flower garden. She told them if she ever found out they'd been fighting—no matter where they were—she would ban them from the house. And he had no doubts that she'd find out.

Khalil raised his hands in surrender. "Damn, Brandon. Relax. You know where to find me if you want to talk about it." He turned and strode off.

He finished his workout and went upstairs to his brother's office. "You never said why you're still here."

Khalil glanced up from his desk. "I lost track of time drawing some designs. Better now?"

Brandon dropped down in the chair. "No," he grumbled. He had worked out over an hour and the only thing he'd successfully done was work up a sweat. He still wanted Faith. Bad.

"Is this the same woman Justin mentioned on Sunday?"

He nodded and told Khalil about the visits and dinners. He groaned. "I can't stop thinking about her."

"She must be something."

"She is. But she's leaving in a week or two."

"That's a good thing, isn't it? You said you weren't looking for anything serious."

He frowned. The thought of her leaving didn't sit well.

Khalil grinned.

"Why are you smiling?"

"No reason." He stood, packed up his papers and locked the desk. "I'm going home."

They walked out and stood in the parking lot talking for a few minutes.

When the conversation ended, Khalil said, "You never answered my question."

Brandon remained silent.

"That's what I thought. Sounds like she means more to you than you expected."

"Yeah. More." With her intelligence, teasing smile and sweet kisses, she was getting to him. And he didn't know how to make it stop.

Chapter 9

Late Friday afternoon, Brandon sat in his office staring out of the window. He'd spent a restless night trying to figure out how to proceed with Faith and decided to go with the flow for now. She'd be gone soon and then he'd move on, as would she. He left his office and went down the hall, wanting to catch Siobhan before she left. She was packing up when he entered.

"Hey, sis. I'm glad I caught you."

"What's up? I hope you don't need anything today. It's almost six and Justin and I are going to a movie."

"No. This has nothing to do with work."

"You ready, baby?" Justin asked, entering. "Oh, hey, Brandon. I didn't know you were here. Are you guys meeting?"

"No. I just came to ask her something. Since you're here, maybe you have an idea, too. Where would you take someone if you wanted to show them the city?" He had never done a sightseeing date. Most of his dates consisted of dinners, fund-raisers, plays or concerts. The women he had dated all lived in LA and touring the city had never been high on his list of things to do. The women, either, for that matter.

Justin leaned against the desk. "Sounds like it's gotten to be more than 'friendly.'"

Siobhan smiled. "I know the perfect place—Santa Monica Pier." She came and stood next to Justin.

Justin nodded and slid his arm around Siobhan's waist. He spoke to Brandon, but his gaze was on his wife. "You have to go in the evening. Black velvet night…millions of stars in the sky…" He nuzzled Siobhan's neck.

"Mmm," Siobhan said.

"A warm breeze," Justin continued, then kissed her.

Brandon frowned. "Can you two knock it off? In case you've forgotten, I'm still standing here. And that is *too* much information."

They both laughed. Siobhan said, "Bye, Brandon. Enjoy your date because I'm definitely going to enjoy mine."

Justin picked up Siobhan's tote and straightened from the desk. "Trust me, Brandon. Go at night."

Brandon followed their departure. He had never seen his sister smile this much or be so relaxed. Until she met Justin, Siobhan had been holding on to a childhood trauma and had spent the next several years trying to make up for something that was never her fault. Brandon was glad she had finally let go of that pain.

He went back to his office to finish up a report. As usual, he was the last to leave. He had initially dismissed Siobhan and Justin's suggestion, but by the time he made it home and finished dinner, began to think it might be a good idea and called Faith to see if she would be interested in spending the day with him.

"What time are you thinking?" Faith asked.

Brandon remembered what Justin had mentioned about

the evening being a better time. "Somewhere around four." With it getting dark later, the time would give her time to see the pier in the daylight and catch the sunset, since she seemed to like that.

"Can we make it five? I'll be spending the first part of the day with my father."

"Sure. We're doing casual so don't worry about dressing up. And wear comfortable shoes."

"That was going to be my next question. Where are we going?"

"Just doing a little sightseeing, nothing big. So, I'll see you tomorrow at five." They spoke a minute longer and he ended the call. Brandon smiled. He wanted to make sure that she never forgot her visit to the city…or him.

Brandon spent Saturday morning tying up all the loose ends of their date. He'd been asking himself all day why he was going through all of this trouble for a casual relationship. He still hadn't come up with an answer.

He readily admitted to liking Faith, but when she opened the door to him that evening and the only thing on his mind was making love to her, he knew there had to be something else going on with him. Not wanting to dwell on it, he pushed aside the thoughts.

"Hey, sweetheart." He made sure their bodies didn't touch when he kissed her because they wouldn't make it out of her place otherwise.

Faith smiled up at him. "Hi. I'm all ready." She locked up and followed him out. On the way, she said, "This will be my first official sightseeing trip and I'm excited."

Brandon smiled, getting caught up in her excitement. As soon as the traffic on the highway slowed to a crawl, he glanced over and met her eyes.

"I didn't say anything." Faith turned and stared out the window, but not before he saw her smile.

"Are we going to the pier?" she asked when it came into view.

"We are." Not bothering to search for parking on the street, he drove into a nearby garage. They strolled along the pier and beach area for a while. Though early evening, the temperature still hovered near eighty degrees. After a while, she stopped and looked out at the water with an expression of contentment on her face. They reversed their course and came back to their starting point.

"I haven't done something like this in a long time, so thank you."

"I'm glad you enjoyed yourself. Are you ready to leave?"

Faith whirled around. "Leave? We aren't going to the amusement park?"

"I hadn't planned on it," he said slowly.

She rolled her eyes. "Brandon, we *have* to go. You can't just come to the pier and not go. Doesn't it look like fun?"

Brandon glimpsed over his shoulder at the big Ferris wheel, roller coasters and the tower ride that dropped a person from a height he didn't even want to think about. *Fun?* He thought not. He didn't do amusement parks, rides and games...or at least he hadn't since his teen years. His type of fun involved silken sheets and soft music.

Faith grabbed him by the arm. "Oh, come on. It'll be fun. We're supposed to be sightseeing and there are lots of *sights* I want to *see*."

Usually, women didn't have a problem with him calling the shots and never questioned where he took them on a date, but not Faith. She'd called him bossy, told him when she didn't care for something he said and now nearly dragged him toward a place he didn't want to go.

When they reached the ticket booth, Faith opened her purse and slid her credit card into the tray. "Two unlimited wrist bands." Before the woman behind the glass could take it, Brandon snatched it.

Brandon scowled down at her. "What do you think you're doing?"

"Paying for the unlimited ride wrist band. What does it look like?" She reached for her card and he moved it out of her grasp. "Brandon."

The woman looked on with amusement.

Faith frowned at him. "You're holding up the line."

Brandon slipped her card into his pocket and withdrew his own. "Two wristbands."

The woman swiped his card, had him sign a receipt and handed him their wristbands. When he walked away, she said to Faith, "Honey, don't be mad at him. I wish I had a man like that. He can take me anywhere," she added with a chuckle.

Faith realized that the woman had a point. Women would kill to have a man who didn't mind footing the bill. She just didn't want him to think she expected him to pay every time they went somewhere. "Can I have my card back now?" He handed it back without a word. "You really should have let me pay, especially since you hadn't planned for us to come here. I don't want you to think I can't pay my way."

He didn't reply immediately. Finally he peered down at her. "I never thought that, Faith. And I don't want to argue."

"Neither do I."

"I promised you fun, so…" Brandon gestured her forward.

Faith enjoyed herself tremendously. They rode the Ferris wheel twice and she talked him into getting on the ocean-front roller coaster that provided a spectacular view of the Pacific Ocean and the bay. She stuffed her face with cotton candy, a funnel cake and a pretzel, and cradled the tiger

Brandon had won in her arms. By the time they walked back to the car, the sun had started to set. "Can we go watch the sunset?"

"Absolutely." He withdrew a blanket from his trunk and they went and found a spot on the beach. He spread it out, sat and pulled her down onto his lap, then slid his arms around her.

She leaned back against his chest and covered his hands with hers. This one was more spectacular than the one she saw at the restaurant. At length, she asked, "Are you angry about going to the park?"

"No. Why?"

"Just wondering. You didn't seem like you were having a good time." Faith angled her head his way. "Do women usually follow wherever you lead?"

Brandon paused before answering. "Usually."

"Hmph. Figured as much."

He tightened his hold. "But I'm finding I like it when a woman takes the lead every now and again. And I did have fun."

They shared a smile and refocused their attention on the now darkening sky. The moon rose, fat and bright, and stars dotted the heavens. "It's a beautiful night."

"Yes. But it doesn't hold a candle to you," he whispered against her ear. Brandon shifted her until she sat sideways and lowered his head.

As always, Faith thought Brandon's kisses were magnificent. His tongue swept into her mouth, hot and demanding. Brandon brought his hand up, cradled her cheek in his palm and continued to kiss her. He gently sucked on her tongue and she felt the pull all the way to her center. Faith tore her mouth away, breathing harshly.

"Take me home, Brandon."

He searched her face. "Are you saying…?"

She leaned up and kissed him softly. "That's exactly what I'm saying."

"But, the other night you said—"

She placed a finger against his lips. "You said you wouldn't make me beg. You promised I wouldn't have to wait."

Before the words were out of her mouth, Brandon surged to his feet with her in his arms and stood her on the sand. He reached down for the blanket, balled it up, grabbed her hand and strode purposefully across the beach and down the block to the parking garage.

Faith studied Brandon as he drove. The tight set of his jaw and the way his hands gripped the steering wheel told her he was fighting for control.

"I really need for there to be no traffic tonight," he said.

So did she. She would be leaving soon for good and wanted to know one time how it felt to be cherished by him. By the time they made it to her place, nervousness claimed her. She usually dated a man much longer before deciding to sleep with him. And, technically, she and Brandon weren't even dating.

Brandon gathered her in his arms. "Change your mind?"

She shook her head. "Not at all."

"I want you to be sure, Faith."

"I'm very sure."

"If you want me to stop—"

"Brandon." She cut him off. "The only thing I want you to stop doing right now is talking."

He chuckled. "Then how about I do this instead?" He tilted her head back and brushed his lips against the exposed column of her neck, along her jaw and her eyelids.

He teased the corners of her mouth with his tongue and dipped inside. His hands toured her shoulders, feathered down her back, and then around to the front to cup her breasts. Faith shuddered, the slow exploration driving her out of her mind.

"You have the softest skin," Brandon murmured, while removing her top. "And these beautiful breasts have been calling me since I left on Thursday." He unclasped her bra and slid the straps down and off. He circled his tongue around first, one nipple, then the other before suckling them.

Faith cried out. She could barely stand. A pulsing began in her core that grew stronger by the second.

He lifted his head. "I think we need to move this to the bedroom."

"I think you might be right." She took his hand and led him back to the room she'd been using. The sensual kisses and roaming hands began again. She pushed his shirt up and over his head, then tossed it aside. She ran her hands over the sculpted planes of his biceps, shoulders and chest, wanting to feel his warm, smooth skin beneath her fingers.

Brandon's eyes closed and he groaned. "I like the way your hands feel on me."

She liked his hands on her, as well. So much so, that when they covered her breasts again, she arched her back to get closer. For the next few minutes, he treated her to sultry kisses, taking his time and driving her out of her mind with desire.

"Brandon," she panted. "Hurry."

"No can do, baby." Brandon dropped to his knees and charted a path with his tongue from the valley between her breasts to her belly button. "I'm going to take my time touching and kissing every part of your body, then make love to you, slowly...thoroughly. I'm going to start here." He stood and stroked a finger down her cheek. "And work my way down your sexy body, turn you around and go up the other side." He spun her around. "Take you from the back," he continued hotly.

Oh. My. Faith melted.

"Then…"

He rotated her to face him again, locked his gaze on her and a wolfish grin played around his lips. "Then, I'm going to do it all over again."

She was halfway to an orgasm just from his sizzling words. If he actually touched her, she would go up in flames.

In the blink of an eye, he removed her shorts and panties, and placed her on the bed. "Shall we begin?"

True to his words, Brandon used his hands and mouth to tease and torment, taking her to the brink of ecstasy, time and time again. He latched on to a hardened nipple and tugged gently, then lavished the same attention on its twin. The kisses moved lower, grazing her core, then continued to her thighs, knees and ankles. Faith felt as if she were coming out of her skin. Never had she experienced such overwhelming sensations.

"Bran… Brandon." She moaned and writhed as he kissed his way up one inner thigh and then the other.

"Do you like that?" Brandon whispered.

She couldn't begin to answer him, not with his talented fingers parting her sensitive folds. He slid one finger inside and she came with a strangled cry. He added another finger, moving them in and out and prolonging the pleasure.

"Damn, baby. You're so wet. I can't wait to get inside you." He withdrew his fingers and kissed her once more. Standing, he undressed, donned a condom and came back to the bed.

Faith had always known his body would be a work of art, but her imagination hadn't come close to the sheer magnificence of this man's physique. She delighted in the feel of him stretched on top of her. She skated her fingers over his broad shoulders and down his back, feeling the muscles contract beneath her touch. "I love this body of yours, Brandon."

"Mmm, and I love the way your bare skin feels against mine." Brandon nudged her legs apart and, holding her gaze, guided himself inside her.

When he was buried to the hilt, they both moaned. He pulled out to the tip and plunged deep. He shuddered and held still for a moment before he started to move in slow insistent circles. He delved deeper with each rhythmic push and Faith wrapped her legs around him and lifted her hips to meet the next powerful thrust.

The sounds of their breathing increased and he set a pace that had the bed rocking. "I knew it would be this way with us," he said. "I can't get enough of you." He tilted her hips, never missing a beat. "I need to be deeper inside you, baby."

Faith held him tighter as the pleasure built, this time even stronger. He gripped her hips tighter and his strokes came faster. Her breath came in short gasps and she convulsed with a loud wail.

Brandon slowed and pulled out. "That's it. Come for me, sweetheart." He gently turned her on her stomach and traced a path down the center of her spine with his tongue. "Now, from behind."

Before she could recover, he surged back in, thrusting high and deep. He placed his thighs over hers, squeezing her legs closed. The sensations were so intense Faith thought she might pass out. It only took a couple of minutes for another blinding climax to overtake her. She screamed even louder.

Brandon pumped harder, went rigid against her and found his own explosive release. His body shuddered and he called her name on a ragged sigh. He collapsed on her, and then shifted to his side, taking her with him.

Faith lay there gulping in air. Her eyes slid closed and

her body still tingled. Several minutes passed before her heart rate slowed.

Brandon turned onto his back and pulled her on top of him. His hand feathered up her spine. "And now we do it again," he whispered huskily.

She gave him a sultry smile. "As long as you allow me the same opportunity to work my way up and down *your* body, we can do it as many times as you like." She took the condom he handed her and rolled it down his engorged length, stroking him as she went.

He sucked in a sharp breath and groaned. "Baby…" He lifted her and brought her down slowly.

As they starting moving, she knew she would never forget this night. Or him.

Chapter 10

Brandon leaned back in his chair, picked up his coffee and rotated toward the window. Although it was Sunday morning, he had gotten up and driven to the office. He sipped slowly while thinking about the day he and Faith had spent yesterday. He couldn't remember the last time he had gone an entire day without doing any work. And he'd had a great time. But it was the memories of what happened after they'd left the beach that had kept him awake and aroused all night. He hadn't expected her to be so uninhibited, especially when she told him she thought it only fair that she get a turn to work her way up and down his body. She had treated him to the most passionate night of his life and given herself totally.

Brandon set the cup on his desk. Too bad he couldn't say the same. As much as he enjoyed the sex, he could not bring himself to surrender his entire being to a woman. Doing so would mean opening up emotions and places within he had purposely locked away to protect his heart.

That was a risk he wouldn't take. However, he wouldn't mind driving over to the hotel for just one more round.

Shaking himself mentally, he turned back to the mounds of paperwork on his desk. He wanted to prove to his father that he was more than ready to take over running the company. If that meant spending his Sunday afternoon working, so be it.

He had been working steadily for more than two hours when his cell chimed. He picked it up and smiled when he saw Faith's name on the display.

Forgot to tell you last night, I'm going home.

Brandon went still. He typed back: For good?

No. Need to check on a few things at home, came the reply.

How long are you going to be gone? he texted.

Not sure.

For a brief moment, something akin to panic settled in his chest. But that couldn't be right. He did not panic over *any* woman. *First time for everything.* He dismissed the notion and replied: When you get back, I have a surprise for you.

What kind of surprise?

You'll have to come back to find out, he typed.

He smiled again. She didn't respond, but he was confident she would be back soon. Another vision of them naked in her bed floated through his mind. Faith had matched him stroke for stroke and fit him better than any other woman. *Whoa.* He didn't like where this line of thinking was headed. Why was he obsessing over one night? He had to keep his mind from traveling to a place it had no business going.

Brandon snatched up the phone again and called Khalil.

"What can I do for you at this ungodly hour, big bro?" Khalil said when he answered.

He chuckled. "It's almost eleven."

"And your point would be? I do like to sleep in every now and again. What if I was entertaining?"

"Boy, please. You like to wake up in your bed *alone* just like I do."

Khalil laughed. "You're right about that. No sense in inviting that kind of drama. So what did you want?"

"For you to open the gym."

He laughed harder. "So this woman is giving you fits, huh?"

Brandon groaned inwardly and muttered, "Something like that."

"Maybe you ought to just sleep with her and stop pretending you're just being friendly. Ain't nothing like a good night of sex to ease your tension."

Except it hadn't eased his tension. It only made it worse. He knew he was setting himself up for Khalil to tease him mercilessly if he confessed to already having slept with Faith, but told him anyway. "We already did."

There was complete silence on the line for several seconds before Khalil said, "I don't believe it. I'll be there in an hour and I want to know all about this woman." He hung up without giving Brandon a chance to reply.

Brandon muttered a curse and pushed to his feet. He straightened his desk, shut down the computer and locked up.

Khalil was getting out of his car when Brandon pulled into the gym's parking lot. Brandon hopped out and the two brothers greeted each other with a one-arm hug.

As soon as they entered the gym, Khalil turned on a light and said, "Spill it."

"Nothing to tell," Brandon said nonchalantly. "We had sex. It was good." Incredible if he were honest, which was the crux of his problem. He had never been so distracted by a woman. Everything about Faith appealed to him, from her enchanting smile to her spirit in the bedroom. Even the fact that she didn't hesitate to call him out or readily agree with whatever he said drew him. Especially that. He put on a pair of boxing gloves and went to the heavy bag.

"Must've been *real* good for you to be in here less than a day later." Khalil took a seat on a nearby bench. "If it was all that, why not just call her up and ask for a repeat tonight?"

"Because she's gone back to Portland," Brandon said between punches.

"Portland?"

"Yeah. That's where she lives."

"So she just left without telling you? Is she coming back?"

"She texted me earlier and said she was." He took a few more punches. "I just don't know when." It had crossed his mind that she might get home and decide not to return. He hit the bag harder, not wanting to analyze why the thought caused his gut to churn.

"I sure hope it's soon. Otherwise, I'll be sending you the bill to replace my equipment."

Brandon eased up on his punches. His arms and shoulders were going to be sore in the morning. He went at the bag for another few minutes, then dropped down on the bench beside his brother. He stripped off the gloves and wiped the sweat from his face.

Khalil handed him a bottle of water. "Better?"

"Not even close," he murmured, twisting off the cap and draining the bottle.

He chuckled. "I'm so glad I don't have these problems. There isn't a woman alive who can make me this crazy. Unless you plan to get serious about this woman, you'd better get control of yourself. The next thing you know, she'll be looking for a ring."

"It'll never come to that. She doesn't live here, remember? And I don't do long-distance relationships. I don't do serious, either. Period. It's just sex." Just because the sex between them had been incredible and he wanted nothing more than to be buried deep inside her while she called his name again didn't mean he wanted exclusivity. That only meant… Hell, he didn't know what it meant.

Faith navigated through the airport and out to the curb. While searching for Kathi, her mind went back to Brandon and what kind of surprise he had in store. Curiosity made her somewhat anxious to get back to LA. That and the prospect of them having another night like the previous one. Her body was still a little sore and she'd noticed several passion marks that morning as she dressed. Thankfully, all of them were in places covered by her clothing. To say it had been something straight out of a fantasy would be a huge understatement, and she'd woken up several times during the night, her body pulsing.

She spotted Kathi's Acura and stepped out to wave her down.

Kathi eased to the curb, popped the trunk and got out. "Hey, girl." They embraced.

"Hey. Thanks for picking me up." Faith put her suitcase and tote in the trunk and slid into the passenger seat.

"How was your flight?" Kathi asked as she merged into the traffic.

"Uneventful." Faith stifled a yawn. Between that second round and the erotic dreams that had plagued her all night, she had only gotten a couple hours of sleep. "How's the new job going?" Kathi had started working as a pharmacist at a local hospital two months ago.

"It's going pretty well. The great thing is that I only have to work one Saturday a month and I'm in the outpatient pharmacy, which closes at six. The inpatient one is twenty-four hours. The other pharmacist is a dream to work with compared to the last one—no snide remarks about me being too young and questioning what I'm doing."

Faith smiled. "I'm so glad it's going well."

Kathi slanted her an amused glance. "Girl, me, too. One more day working with that old geezer and I might have fed him that Bengay he always smelled like."

She frowned. "Eww, the image I'm getting." They burst out laughing.

"I know, right. Anyway, how are things with you and Brandon?"

Loaded question. "There's no me and Brandon, but things are fine." If she were in the market for a relationship, he'd top the list. But since she wasn't, things were getting more complicated by the minute. "He took me to Santa Monica Pier and to the amusement park yesterday."

"Sounds like fun."

"It was." From walking on the pier, playing games and going on the rides to sitting on the beach watching the sunset, everything about the evening had be amazing. Not to mention what happened afterward. Never had she had a more perfect date. Faith gave her an update on Thad.

"Is your mom still mad?"

"I have no idea. We haven't really spoken much."

As they pulled into Faith's complex, Kathi said, "I've been keeping an eye on the place. Your mail is stacked on the kitchen counter."

"I can't tell you how much I appreciate you."

"Do you know when you're going back?"

Faith sighed. "No. I'm thinking the weekend. I'll let

you know what I decide. Today, I'll probably go over to my parents' house."

"Guess you'll be having that conversation with your mom sooner rather than later."

"Yeah." And she wasn't looking forward to the confrontation. She climbed out of the car, retrieved her luggage and waved. "I'll call you."

"Okay. Let me know how it goes with your mom."

Faith nodded. She unlocked her door, stepped inside her condo and released a deep breath, happy to be home. She glanced around to make sure everything was in its place and smiled.

She made her way to her bedroom, left the suitcase and tote by the door, and flopped down on the bed. "My bed." She sighed heavily. She'd missed being in her own space. Faith allowed herself a few more minutes of relaxation, then scooted off the bed and started the task of unpacking and doing laundry.

While her clothes were in the wash, she went through the huge stack of mail that had accumulated in her absence and paid her bills. Once she finished putting away the clothes, she took a quick shower and set out for her parents' house. She had put off talking to her mother for almost a month, but now it was time.

Twenty minutes later, Faith parked behind her mother's car in the driveway. Part of her had hoped they weren't home. She drew in a fortifying breath and got out. The front door opened before she made it halfway up the walk and her stepfather rushed to meet her with his arms spread wide. Though he stood only five-nine, his slim build and ramrod spine made him seem taller.

"Hey, baby girl. You're back."

"Hi, Daddy," she said, moving into his embrace.

He eased back and studied her critically. "How are you doing? Anything still bothering you from the accident?"

She shook her head. "No. I'm good as new."

He released her and they continued up the walkway. "When did you get back?"

"Earlier today."

He held the door open. "You should've called. I would've picked you up."

Faith smiled. "I know. Kathi offered to come get me." She followed him to the living room, steeling herself for her mother's response.

"Francis, look who's back," her stepfather said.

Faith's mother slowly closed the book she had been reading. "Hello, Faith." She smoothed a hand over her shoulder-length dark hair. She'd added a few more strands of gray hair since Faith had seen her a month ago.

"Hi, Mom." She perched on the edge of the sofa and her father claimed his favorite recliner. Her mother looked tired.

After several seconds, her mother asked, "How was your trip?"

"Enlightening." Her mother fiddled with the bookmark and Faith glanced over at her father.

He sighed, shook his head and stood. "Faith, I hope you'll stay for dinner. I'm doing some pork chops on the grill," he added, knowing she would never turn down anything he cooked.

A smile curved her lips. "You know I will."

"Good." He patted her shoulder and divided a wary look between the two women, then left.

Faith and her mother sat in strained silence for a few moments.

"You seem to have recovered from the accident. I'm glad."

She nodded. "I have."

"Did you meet him?" her mother asked softly.

"Yes. He's a very nice man and I enjoyed talking to him."

"So, what does that mean for…for us?"

Faith frowned. "I don't understand."

Her mother looked away.

Finally, it dawned on her. "Are you talking about you and Daddy?"

She nodded hesitantly.

"Mom, nothing has changed. You're still my parents and I love you." She came and hunkered next to her mother. "But Thad is my father and I want to know him, too."

Her mother swiped at a tear and whispered brokenly, "I know he hates me for what I've done."

"He doesn't hate you." Faith thought about her and Thad's conversation. She still marveled at his ability to let go. "He did say he was angry for a long time and I'm sure you can understand why. But he has forgiven you and said we can only move forward."

"And you?"

"I'm not going to lie, Mom, I am still a little angry, but I'm working on it."

"I'm sorry, Faith."

"So am I, Mom."

She grasped Faith's hand. "I want you to know that I loved your father. He is a *good* man, but I just couldn't deal with what was happening to him."

Faith tried to put herself in her mother's shoes. She had never been around anyone with PTSD, but had read stories and guessed it would be frightening to see someone you loved going through something so horrible. "He seems to be doing pretty well in that area, but he did sustain an injury that required a lower left leg amputation."

Her mother gasped and brought her hand to her mouth.

Faith shared what Thad had told her. "I'm just sad that he never remarried or had any other children." She rose, went to retrieve her cell phone and brought up the picture she'd taken of them together. She handed it to her mother.

"He hasn't aged a day. I didn't realize how much you favor him."

She chuckled. "It was kind of weird at first." She accepted the phone back and stared at the photo. Their smiles were nearly identical. "He's asked me to visit a while longer."

"Are you going back to LA soon?"

"Most likely. Maybe for another two or three weeks." When Faith had called Thad to tell him she was going home, she could hear the fear in his voice—that she would be gone from his life again. Faith had assured him that she would be back. His sigh of relief had tempted her to cancel her flight.

"How long do you plan to be home before you go back?"

She shrugged. "A week or so. I have a few things I need to take care of. But I'll be sure to let you guys know when I'm leaving."

"Thank you."

Faith observed her mom and read uncertainty in her features. Did her mother really think Faith would leave without saying goodbye? And was there still some doubt that Faith would discard her now that Faith had been reunited with Thad? Granted, Faith still had some lingering annoyance, but as Thad had pointed out, she couldn't change the past. Hoping to allay her mother's concerns, she said, "I'll probably book a flight for next Monday. That'll give me a week to finish things and come back to spend time with you and Dad."

Her mother's eyes lit up. "We'd like that."

They shared a smile and went to see how dinner was coming along.

After returning home later that evening, Faith sent a text to Brandon letting him know she made it home, and then called Kathi. Kathi had invited Faith to a July Fourth picnic to be held that week, but Faith declined.

She spent most of the week taking care of bank business, meeting with two local clients and preparing herself to be gone another three weeks. She had checked her budget and determined that was the maximum time she could be away without having to dip into her savings. She'd plan another visit for later in the year, or maybe Thad could come to Portland. She would enjoy showing him around.

Sunday evening, Faith started the task of packing. She stood in her closet pulling out clothes more suited for the warmer LA temperatures, as well as selecting a couple of nice dresses just in case she and Brandon went out again. Brandon. She hadn't talked to him since he'd responded to her text a week ago. Memories of their times together surfaced in her mind, along with his promise of a surprise. She hoped it entailed another round in the bedroom. The way he touched her, held her, kissed her… Her cell phone rang, snapping her out of her lustful thoughts. She laid the dresses on her bed and answered.

"Hello."

"Hi, Faith. It's Thad. How are you?"

"Hi, Thad. I'm good."

"I was calling to see when you'd be coming back to LA."

"I'll be flying in tomorrow. Is there anything wrong?" There was a pause on the line and a small measure of fear crept into her brain. Her first thought was his leg. Had something happened?

"There's nothing wrong, but I need to discuss something important with you."

"You're not sick or anything?" They had just reconnected. She didn't know how she would handle the prospect of him having an illness.

Thad chuckled. "No, sweetheart. I plan to be around for a long while. Do you think we can talk this week?"

"Of course. Since I'm not getting in until late afternoon, what about Tuesday or Wednesday?"

"Wednesday works fine. I can meet you at the hotel."

"No, that's okay. I'd rather come to your house."

"I'll throw in dinner. How's that?"

Faith smiled. "Sounds great." They talked a few minutes longer to finalize the details and ended the call. She lightly tapped the phone against her chin and wondered what he wanted to discuss. First, Brandon and his surprise, now this.

Tossing the phone aside, she went back to packing. She was anxious to find out what Thad had to say. And to see Brandon.

Chapter 11

Wednesday evening, Faith rang Thad's doorbell precisely at seven thirty.

Thad opened the door and had a huge smile on his face. "You're right on time. Come on in."

She followed him to the kitchen and placed the box she had been carrying on the counter.

He set one crutch aside and maneuvered to the stove to stir something in a pot.

She sniffed. "Whatever you're cooking smells really good."

He glanced over his shoulder. "I should've asked you what you liked. I've got some fried catfish, potato salad, beans and…" He removed a pan from the oven. "Corn-bread."

Faith's mouth watered. "Mmm, I can't wait." She hadn't had fried fish in a long while. Growing up, her mother had cooked fish on most Fridays. Faith remembered asking why and her mother saying it was something her mother had done.

Thad gestured. "What's in the box?"

"I thought since you were cooking dinner, I'd contribute dessert."

He grinned and his eyebrows shot up. "Yeah? What did you bring?"

"I just made a yellow cake with chocolate frosting." Since the hotel had a full kitchen, she had decided to bake the cake instead of buying one from the store.

His smile widened. "I may have to skip dinner and go straight for dessert. How did you know that was my absolute favorite cake?"

Faith laughed. "It's mine, too."

Thad shook his head and turned away briefly.

She saw him discreetly wiping at his face. She rounded the island and placed a comforting hand on his shoulder. She understood. How many more things did they have in common? "Like you said, we can only go forward."

He nodded.

She wrapped her arms around his waist and laid her head on his shoulder. He held her tight.

After a moment, he released her. "We'd better eat before the food gets cold."

They fixed their plates and sat at the kitchen table. He recited a blessing and she dug in. The fish tasted so good she groaned. She held up a piece. "You have *got* to tell me what seasonings you used. I haven't had fish this good in years."

He took a sip of his iced tea. "I'm glad you're enjoying it."

Faith was more than enjoying her food. She didn't eat everybody's potato salad, but tonight she had two helpings. She studied him as he got up to get another piece of cornbread, marveling at how easily he maneuvered with

one crutch. "You mentioned being fitted for another prosthesis. Any word on when it might be ready?"

Thad returned to his seat. "I'm hoping it'll be ready in
another couple of weeks, but who knows."

Faith listened as Thad told her about the process.

Then he abruptly changed the subject. "How did it go
with your mother?"

She wiped her hands. "Okay, I guess. We talked, so
that's a plus."

"I'm glad." He pointed to her empty plate. "There's
plenty more if you want."

She held up a hand. "No, thank you. If I eat one more
bite, I won't be able to move from this chair. Everything
was delicious. Besides, I need to save room for a little bitty
piece of cake," she added with a wink.

Thad laughed and patted his stomach. "Need to save
some space myself."

She paused briefly, then said, "You mentioned wanting
to talk to me about something important."

He nodded. "We can talk in the family room. And I'm
going to have a piece of that cake."

Faith rose from the table and took their dishes to the
sink. "If you show me where the plates and silverware
are, I'll cut you a piece and bring it in." He pointed out the
cabinet and drawers and left her to the task. She cut two
slices of the cake, added forks and carried them to where
he sat in the same recliner as he had on her first visit. She
handed him the larger piece.

A smile blossomed on his face. "Now, that's what I'm
talking about."

She laughed. "You might want to hold off until you
taste it."

He forked up a large bite and chewed. His eyes slid
closed and he groaned with delight. "Baby girl, I may

have to ask for one of these monthly. Although my doctor won't agree."

"I'm glad you like it. How about we make it bimonthly? That way you'll have plenty of time to work it off in between."

Thad chuckled. "That's a deal I can live with." He toasted her with his fork and went back to his cake. A minute later, he set the plate aside, picked up a check from the side table and handed it to her.

Faith looked at it and her eyes widened. "What's this for?"

"You've spent a lot of money between flying and staying at that hotel. I would've loved to have you stay here, but I didn't know how comfortable you'd be, so you take that."

He had been correct about the costs, but the amount on the check in her hand could cover what she'd spent three times over. "But—"

He shook his head. "No buts. I never meant for you to pay in the first place. I had planned to send for you when and if you called."

"I… I don't know what to say."

Thad picked up his plate. "You can just say thank you and eat your cake." That said, he went back to his half-eaten cake.

"Thank you." Still stunned, she smiled and finished eating. When they were done, she stood and reached for his plate. "I'll take these to the kitchen. Is that what you wanted to talk to me about?"

"Partly."

Faith stopped, turned back and noted his serious expression. "Okay," she said slowly. "I'll be right back." As she stacked the plates, she tried to figure out what else he might say. He had told her he wasn't ill, but maybe he hadn't wanted to tell her over the phone. She came back and reclaimed her spot on the sofa.

Thad leaned forward and clasped his hands together. "I'm going to retire soon—in the next few weeks, actually—and I have a proposal for you to consider."

"All right."

"Maybe I should start from the beginning. I told you that the company where I worked was started by my best friend and that he invited me to join him as vice president."

She nodded.

"Well, at that time we decided that the company would always remain in our families, with a Gray at the helm as CEO and a Whitcomb as VP."

Faith sat up straight. "Are you saying...?"

Thad nodded. "Yes. I want you to succeed me as vice president, as well as occupy my seat on the board. Nolan and I will remain on as advisors, but his oldest son will take his seat and you, mine."

She rose to her feet and paced, trying to process what he'd said. "I don't know anything about the home safety business."

He shrugged. "Maybe not now, but you're an intelligent young woman who started her own business, so I have no doubts that you'll be able to learn what you need to know. And I'll be here to help you."

She dropped back down on the sofa. Several things had crossed her mind, but no way could she have imagined this.

"This is your legacy, Faith. I prayed and prayed that I would have the opportunity to pass it on to you."

His voice cracked and she sensed his emotions rising again. She felt herself on the brink of agreeing, but pushed it down. She had too much at stake. "I understand. I'm honored and...frankly speechless. What about my business? I don't know how I'd be able to do both and I can't just give up what I've worked so hard to build. Then there's my living arrangements. My home and my life are in Portland." She threw her hands up. "I'd have to give up everything."

Thad came and sat next to her. He grasped her hands. "Honey, I know what I'm asking is a lot, especially since we're still trying to get to know each other. All I ask is that you think about it. Please."

His eyes pleaded with her and, once again, she was tempted to agree just to make him happy. "I promise, I will."

"I'd also like to introduce you to Nolan and his family, as well as the other board members at the next meeting."

Faith felt as if her head was spinning and she desperately wanted to lie down. "But what if I decide not to take the position?"

"I'd still like for them to meet you. Nolan saw you once when you were a baby. After your mom left with you, I don't know what I would have done had it not been for him and his wife, DeAnna. They prayed as hard as I did and are anxious to see you."

She didn't know what to say. But she was glad he'd had someone to help him through that time. "Okay. I'll let you know as soon as I can."

He handed her a business card. "You can go to the website and check out the company, see what it's all about."

She nodded and stood. "I'm going to head out." She had planned to stay long enough to help with the dishes, but right now she needed to think.

Thad followed suit. "Are you going to be okay?"

"Yes. Just feeling a bit overwhelmed at the moment." Faith stuck the card and check into her purse and started toward the front door. "I'll leave the cake for you."

"Thank you. I'm going to do my best not to eat it all tonight." At the door, he gave her a strong hug. "You call me if you have any questions or if you just want to talk."

"I will. Good night." What had started as a quest to find her father had now turned into something much more complicated.

* * *

Thursday morning, Brandon sat at his desk smiling at the text he'd sent Faith. No matter how hard he tried to deny it, he missed her. He'd wanted to go to her place last night, but she was visiting her father. In the twelve days since he'd seen her, visions of her naked body pressed against his had plagued him every night. His cell chimed.

Tonight sounds great. Does this have anything to do with that surprise you promised?

Tonight won't be long enough for what I have in mind, he replied.

Oh.

Brandon chuckled. No, he needed far more time. He typed back: If you're not busy Saturday…

A couple of minutes later, she replied: I'm not.

A slow grin made it across his face and his groin stirred with anticipation. He rotated in his chair and turned his attention back to his emails.

Brandon clicked on one from his father. *An emergency meeting at noon?* When Brandon had seen his father earlier, he hadn't mentioned anything. He glanced at the top and saw that the memo had gone to him and all of his siblings. No other company employees or board members. "Why would he call a meeting without the other staff?" he mumbled. Unless something was wrong with his father or mother. He checked the time. Two hours to wait. Brandon thought about going down to his father's office to ask, but figured it would be a waste of time and his father would be just as closemouthed as he'd been regarding the transition.

Brandon tried to concentrate on the many tasks in front

of him, but his mind kept straying to the meeting and speculating on what was going on.

At fifteen minutes before eleven, he left his office and made his way to the conference room. His baby sister, Morgan, was already there and typing on her iPad.

Morgan lifted her head. "Hey, Brandon."

"Hey, sis." He leaned down, placed a kiss on her temple and slid into the chair next to her. "How's the sports management world coming?"

"I just picked up another player," she said with a bright smile. "That makes six."

He nodded. "I'm proud of you, girl." When she had first expressed a desire to be a sports agent, Brandon had been skeptical about her ability to break into the male-dominated field, especially since she was so young, with only two years of law experience. But now, at twenty-eight, Morgan had not only broken into the field, she'd shattered the wall.

"Thanks." She shut down her iPad. "Do you know what the meeting is about?"

"That's what I'd like to know," Malcolm said, entering with Khalil.

Brandon shook his head. "I have no idea."

Siobhan breezed through the door and greeted everyone. Malcolm rounded the table and pulled her chair out. "Thanks, baby brother."

He kissed her cheek. "You're welcome. How're you feeling?"

She smiled. "Pretty good, now that the morning sickness has passed. Anybody know why we're here?"

They all shrugged.

Khalil said, "I hope this isn't some announcement about Mom or Dad being sick."

Siobhan shook her head. "I just talked to Mom yesterday. She didn't mention anything about not feeling well and she sounded fine."

Brandon leaned back in his chair. "I hope you're right."

"Good. You're all here." They all turned at the sound of their father's voice. Nolan Gray closed the door and took his seat at the head of the table. "I know you all are wondering why I called this meeting, so I'll get right to it. Thad and I will be retiring effective the last Friday of this month." He shifted his gaze to Brandon. "Brandon, starting Monday, you and I will begin your transition. We'll also put things in place to start interviewing for your current position.

Brandon nodded and relief filled him. And he already had someone in mind for his job.

His father leaned forward. "I'm also happy to announce that the vice president position, as well as Thad's seat on the board, will be filled by a Whitcomb heir, just as we had always hoped."

There was stunned silence for a full minute, then the room exploded with questions.

"Uncle Thad has a child?"

"Who is it?"

"Why haven't we ever met his kids?"

Brandon's chest tightened until he felt light-headed. Was he going to be expected to train this guy? And why come out of the woodworks after all this time? All of his siblings' eyes were on him. He clenched his teeth and he gripped the chair arms so hard it was a wonder they didn't break.

"Yes, Thad has a child. It's a long story that I'll leave him to share. Introductions will be made at the next advisory board meeting in two weeks."

Brandon stared at his father in disbelief. "Why now?"

His father sighed. "As I said, Brandon, it's a long story. This changes nothing for you, son."

He pushed to his feet angrily. "It changes everything."

He stalked out. Brandon had been there since he was a teen and knew every inch of the business. He couldn't believe his father expected him to spend precious time training someone who had never set foot in the company.

To keep from saying something he would regret, he avoided talking to his siblings and his father for the rest of the afternoon. The only bright spot was that he'd be seeing Faith in a while.

Brandon reached the hotel close to seven. She had booked the same place and her ground floor room was only two doors down from the original one. When she opened the door, he barely said hello before hauling her into his arms and crushing his mouth against hers in an urgent kiss. She came up on tiptoe to meet him stroke for stroke. He lifted her in his arms, kicked the door shut and carried her across the room to the sofa. The longer he kissed her, the more he began to feel. An unnamed emotion stirred within him and he broke the kiss.

"Mmm, hello to you, too," Faith said.

Holding her in his arms and looking into the face that haunted his nights, Brandon realized he had missed her more than he cared to admit. "Hi, sweetheart." He lowered his head again, unable to get enough of kissing her. At length, he eased back. "How was your trip home?"

She made a move to leave his lap, but he tightened his arms to stay her. She stared at him a moment, then relaxed against his shoulder. "I got a lot accomplished."

"Did you and your mother talk?"

"Yep. We're working through it." She sat up. "Do you want something to eat or drink?"

"No, thanks." He had originally planned to stay longer, but his mood had soured thanks to his dad's little bombshell.

"Is everything okay?"

Brandon frowned. "Yeah, why?"

"I don't know. I heard something in your voice."

He studied her. What did that mean? He hadn't heard anything. And only two other people could read him that well—Khalil and Siobhan. But they'd known him his whole life. How could this woman whom he'd met a month ago seem to know him so well?

"It sounded like you were bothered by something, that's all."

He leaned his head against the back of the sofa and closed his eyes briefly. Maybe talking to her would help. "There's some work stuff going on that has me frustrated."

She scooted off his lap and onto the sofa. "You're not in danger of losing your job, are you?" she asked with concern.

"No, nothing like that."

Something like relief crossed her features. "I'm really glad to hear that. I didn't want you taking off for me to cause you trouble. Are you having problems with your boss?"

Brandon hesitated a beat. "Actually, I'm the boss and will be taking over as CEO of the company at the end of the month."

Faith angled her head. Her eyebrows knit in confusion. "Excuse me, but exactly how is that frustrating? Most people would kill to be in your position. Unless you don't want the job," she added.

"Oh, I want it. I've worked my butt off for seventeen years waiting to get it. And now some unknown person is going to come in and be second-in-command." He wished he knew something…*anything* about this guy. All prospective employees went through a routine background check, but Brandon planned to be more thorough this time.

"I still don't understand."

"I expected to run the company solo, and that's how I want it. I just learned that a person who hasn't spent one day at this company is to be my right hand. I don't have the time or inclination to train someone to do a job he doesn't deserve and one I can do alone."

"So, from what you're saying, the current CEO is bringing in a person to be your second-in-command, right?"

"Yes."

"But, you'll be the CEO, so even if this person is there, *you* will still have the last word on any decisions." Faith shrugged. "And who knows, he may have something to contribute."

That wasn't what Brandon wanted to hear. "So, I'm supposed to just welcome this person in and let him decide the future of *my* company?"

She lifted a brow. "You don't need to get so snippy, Brandon. All I'm saying is you should try to give this guy a chance before you decide his worth." She smiled. "Obviously, the current CEO thinks he's okay, so maybe it won't be so bad." She reached for his hand.

He jumped to his feet. "I don't expect you to understand what it's like to work your entire adult life for something, only to have the reins to be divided at the last minute."

Faith slowly came to her feet and glared at him. "What I don't understand is your attitude." She strode across the room and opened the door. "Maybe you should leave."

Brandon scrubbed a hand down his face. He hadn't meant to take out his anger and irritation on her. "Faith, I—"

"Just go."

He opened his mouth to apologize.

She held up a hand. "Leave. Please."

Rather than dig himself into a deeper hole, he sighed with regret and did as she asked. This was exactly why he kept his dating life fluid—two or three dates and move on—and the expectations stated up front. That way *feelings* and *emotions* never came into play. Brandon had no idea how this thing with Faith had gotten so out of hand. Instead of the short fling they'd agreed upon, something else was growing and he couldn't make it stop. However, he did owe Faith an apology. He just hoped she'd give him the chance.

Chapter 12

Friday, Faith sat staring at her computer screen. She had been working on the same page for over two hours, but couldn't concentrate for more than a few minutes. Brandon's sharp words played over and over in her head. And no matter how much she tried to deny it, she'd been hurt by them. Pushing her feelings aside, she refocused on updating the events page for one of her clients. She had only been working five minutes when her cell rang. Hoping it wasn't Brandon, she picked up the phone and relaxed upon seeing Kathi's name.

"Hey, girl."

"Hey, Faith. I'm sorry I didn't get a chance to call you back yesterday. It's been a little crazy around here."

"No problem. Are you on your lunch break?"

"Yep. And I want to know what your father said."

Faith relayed the details of her and Thad's conversation, including him giving her the check and his job offer.

"I was so stunned I could barely think. I'm still trying to process it all."

"Wow, vice president. That's unbelievable."

"Tell me about it. And a seat on the board." She still couldn't believe it herself.

"You know that would mean you'd have to move to LA," Kathi said. "Are you going to do it?"

Faith blew out a long breath. "I have no idea. It would mean turning my whole life upside down. I told him I'd think about it, but I don't know anything about home safety."

She chuckled. "Maybe not, but for a VP salary, I'd learn real quick."

"I bet you would," she said with a little laugh. "Seriously though, my head is all over the place right now and I'm confused. If I do this, I'm worried about how my parents are going to feel, especially my mom. She's just beginning to accept me having a relationship with Thad. She'll probably freak out if I say I'm moving and succeeding him at his company."

"There is that, but it's your life and it's not like they can't visit."

"True." Faith could just imagine the blowup. She and her mother had come to a truce of sorts, but this could potentially start another feud, one Faith wasn't sure she wanted to initiate.

"Do you know what kind of stuff the company manufactures? And what's the name of it?"

"No to both questions. Thad gave me his business card and asked me to check it out, but I was so overwhelmed that I just stuck it in my purse without looking at it. And I got a little sidetracked last night. I do plan to check it out later today."

Kathi sighed dreamily. "I so wish stuff like this would

happen to me. Anyway, I need to finish lunch and get back to work. Keep me posted."

"I will."

"For what it's worth, I think you should go for it. I'm sure you'd be able to continue your business on the side, just like you were doing before. Not to mention, I'd have a permanent vacation spot. Just saying."

Faith smiled. "Only you, Kathi. Bye, girl." Before she could set the phone down, it rang again. Her smile faded. Brandon. She debated whether to answer or let it go to voice mail like she had done last night. It rang twice more. She heaved a deep sigh and answered.

"I know I'm the last person you want to talk to right now," Brandon said before she could utter a greeting. "But please don't hang up, Faith."

"What can I do for you Brandon?" She tried to remain unmoved by his sincere plea.

"I want to apologize for all the things I said last night. I had no right to take my frustrations out on you. I—"

"No, you did not," she said bluntly, cutting him off. She had done nothing to deserve his tirade and she wasn't giving him a pass.

He sighed heavily. "You're not going to make this easy, are you?"

"Why should I?"

"Faith," he started again.

"Look, Brandon. I know you're used to women falling all over you, letting you get away with saying whatever you please, then accepting a half-assed apology. Well, I'm not one of them."

"No, you're not," Brandon said quietly. "And if you'd let me get a word in, I'd like to try to make things right."

"Go ahead," she mumbled, slouching down in the chair and folding her arms.

"Thank you. I am truly sorry for my harsh words.

Believe me, baby, they were never meant for you. Sometimes—well, all the time if you ask my family," he added with a wry chuckle, "I tend to speak without thinking. I'm really trying to work on it. Faith, you are unlike any woman I have ever met and I don't want to mess up what's happening between us."

Faith sat up straight. What did he mean by that? There wasn't anything happening between them, was there? Granted, her feelings for him had been growing from the moment she woke up in the hospital and saw him sitting in the chair, but did he have feelings for her, as well?

"Please forgive me."

How in the world was she supposed resist when he was playing dirty with that sexy voice and earnest confession? "Okay."

"I can't promise I won't shove my foot in my mouth again, but I will try." Silence rose between them. "So, does this mean we're still on for tomorrow evening?"

She had forgotten about their date. "Yes. And that surprise better be good. *Better* than good."

Brandon burst out laughing. "Sweetheart, you have my word. It will be better than good."

As much as Faith wanted to stay mad, she couldn't.

"I need to get back to work. I'll see you tomorrow."

"All right."

"And, Faith?"

"Yes."

"Thank you for giving me another chance."

Faith held the phone against her heart, lowered her head and closed her eyes. His softly spoken words echoed through her. She was getting in too deep with this man.

Pushing thoughts of Brandon out of her mind, she went to retrieve Thad's business card from her purse. She couldn't concentrate on work and talking with Kathi had roused her curiosity more. She typed in the web address and the company's home page materialized on the screen. The transition between pages was smooth and the site very user-friendly. She was grudgingly impressed. Faith went back to the "About Us" page to learn more about the people behind the company. Nolan Gray, the company's CEO, was a handsome older gentleman with an impressive résumé. He'd come a long way from the garage-based company he'd started.

She scrolled down, saw Thad's photo and smiled. It was obvious that their web design team updated the staff photos often because he looked exactly as he did when she'd seen him two nights ago. Faith continued down the page to the Director of Home Safety and her fingers froze on the track pad.

"Oh, no." She closed her eyes and opened them again, hoping the image on the screen would change. It didn't. There, looking as handsome as ever in a dark tailored suit and perched on the edge of a large mahogany desk was Brandon.

Faith brought her hands to her face and a sick feeling bubbled in her stomach. *She* was the one he thought would come in and take over. The one who knew nothing about *his* company and the one he would have to train. Another thought hit her. Brandon had mentioned when they first met that he worked for a home safety company. Why hadn't she put two and two together? Because he didn't seem to like talking about his job, she had just dismissed it. She groaned. *Just great!* No way would she take the VP position now. How would she explain it to her father? She had seen the hope in his eyes. And Brandon, knowing how he felt, how was she going to tell him?

Brandon wrapped up his meeting with the production manager, glad to know that numbers for the new pressure mattresses had increased. He was especially happy to hear that despite the hiccup with the rails eighteen months ago, those numbers were on the rise, as well. He thanked the woman and rose when she did to walk her to the door. He closed it behind her and went back to his desk.

Thoughts of his earlier conversation with Faith floated through his mind. He'd told her that she was unlike any other woman he had known and he'd meant it. Brandon had never begged a woman—he always found it easier to walk away—but he had come close with Faith. Why her? He shook his head. She had read him up one way and down the other and called his initial attempt to apologize *half-assed*. Then expected his surprise to better than good. *Damn. What a woman.* He planned to take her to his house and prepare dinner, but after messing up with her he needed to step up his game. And he knew just what to do.

Brandon picked up the receiver and called Khalil. Ten minutes later, he hung up confident that what he had in mind would far exceed *better than good.* He still couldn't believe that he had said the things he had. But she had struck a nerve when she told him to wait and see, and that if the current CEO thought the new guy wasn't not too bad, it should be okay. She had no way of knowing that the current CEO was his father and that he and his uncle Thad knew more than they were letting on.

He still couldn't wrap his mind around the fact that his uncle had a kid. Other than the woman he remembered seeing Uncle Thad with at the warehouse that summer, no other one came to mind. Did they have a child together? He and his brothers had spent many nights at their uncle's house and not once had he mentioned having children. There had been no weekend or holiday visits. And Brandon would know because Uncle Thad had spent most of those times with Brandon's family.

Brandon had tried to ask his father again for more details, but got the same answer he'd given at the meeting:

"Thad will share when he's ready." In the meantime, his father expected Brandon to waste time he didn't have. He already had to interview and train his replacement, as well as make his own preparations in taking over for his father. The anger and resentment that had been hovering below the surface rose again and he drew in several deep breaths to gain control of his emotions.

"Knock, knock."

Brandon lifted his head. "Hey, Vonnie. Come on in."

Siobhan eyed him.

"Don't start." Siobhan took her role as the oldest seriously and would stage an intervention if she felt one of her siblings needed it, whether they wanted one or not. The look on her face told him it was coming.

She sat across from him and smiled. "Okay. You get a reprieve for the moment, but only because I have something more urgent. We're planning Dad and Uncle Thad's retirement party and since they've given us such a short window to work with, I want to get the invitations out by Monday afternoon. It's going to be the last Friday of July, which gives us a good three weeks for folks to get their invites. I talked to Malcolm and they don't have to report to camp until that Sunday, so he and Omar are free. I was also thinking—"

Brandon felt a headache coming on. His sister was in full PR and planning mode. "Vonnie, I'm not in the mood to be talking about a party right now."

Siobhan skewered him with a look. "You don't have to be. All you need to do is show up and handle your part, which includes giving the toast. Now, as I was saying…"

He half listened to all the details and wondered how she had found time to do all of this when their father had only announced it yesterday.

"You should bring Faith."

He promptly tuned back in. "What?"

"I said you should bring Faith. That is her name right… the woman from the accident?"

Brandon didn't recall telling his sister Faith's name.

"Justin mentioned her name once."

"As I said before, we're not in that kind of relationship. Besides, she'll probably be gone back home by then." Something else he didn't want to think about. But he'd just said they weren't in a relationship, so it shouldn't bother him if she left. Yet, it did.

"Oh? Hmm… Did you decide to take her to the pier like Justin and I suggested?"

Images of that evening surfaced and Brandon couldn't stop his body's response. Thankfully he was seated behind his desk. "Yes, since I couldn't come up with anything else," he said casually.

Siobhan observed him for a moment, and then smiled. "Well now."

His brow lifted. "Well now, what?"

She stood. "I'll send you everything once I'm done." She walked to the door and turned back. "And, I'll put you down for one plus a guest. I have no doubts about your power of persuasion." She tossed him a bold wink and exited.

Brandon groaned. He didn't know who was worse, Siobhan or Khalil. He did know that he needed that persuasive power for tomorrow.

Chapter 13

Saturday morning, Faith paced back and forth while waiting for Brandon to arrive, far too excited about spending the day with him. Ever since he'd mentioned not wanting to mess up whatever was happening between them, she had wondered what he meant. Did he want them to explore something other than their agreed-upon casual affair? She thought it best to keep her emotions out of it, especially with what she knew. She still hadn't figured out how to broach the subject. Faith checked her watch. He'd said he would arrive at quarter to nine, so she still had a few minutes to come up with something.

She toyed with telling him as soon as he arrived to get it over with, but a selfish part of her looked forward to seeing him and wanted this time. Maybe a better time would be at the end of the date. A knock at the door broke into her thoughts.

Faith went to open the door. Brandon stood there wearing a pair of black shorts and a pale blue short-sleeved button-down shirt, and smiling. "Good morning."

"Morning." Brandon bent and kissed her tenderly.

Any thoughts she had of coming clean fled. If she could bottle up his kisses to take home, she would.

"Are you ready?"

Faith nodded. She picked up her purse, jacket and the bag with an extra set of clothes that he had asked her to bring when he called late last night. He eased it from her hand and she followed him out to his car. As they merged onto the freeway, she was pleasantly surprised to see the traffic flowing at the speed limit. "So, where are we going?"

Brandon slanted her a quick glance. "It's a surprise, remember? If I tell you, then it won't be."

She twisted in her seat to face him. "Oh, that's how you're gonna be?"

He chuckled. "Yep. You said I had to step up my game and give you a *better* than good date. I'm just trying to oblige you." He wiggled his eyebrows and unleashed that smile on her. "I hope you're ready for some fun."

She returned his smile and poked him in the shoulder. "Okay. I'll play your little game, but you'd better bring it. I want to remember this day long after I go home." At the mention of her leaving, the playful mood changed and they fell silent. Faith straightened in her seat and stared out the window. She didn't understand why the thought of leaving bothered her. Even if she came back to visit Thad later in the year, Brandon would have moved on, especially when she came clean about her identity. And she'd be a distant memory. If he remembered her at all.

"How long are you going to be here?"

"About two and a half weeks." She had originally planned to stay two weeks and leave the day after the Gray Home Safety board meeting. However, Thad had convinced her to stay through the weekend because he wanted to have some kind of welcome party for her. He seemed sure the Gray family would welcome her with open arms, but she knew differently and questioned whether the gathering would be a good idea.

Brandon reached for her hand and brought it to his lips. "Then we have plenty of time." He smiled.

Faith returned his smile, but inside knew that time was running out. A short while later, they reached Long Beach and she saw a sign that read The Catalina Landing. "A cruise?"

"Yes, ma'am. We're going to take a trip to Catalina Island." He tossed her a bold wink and hopped out of the car.

She groaned inwardly. If this was his definition of stepping up his game, she was in trouble. He came around and helped her out of the car. Without letting go of her hand, he shut the door, pressed the remote locks and started off.

"Wait. Don't I need my bag?"

He stopped and looked down at her. "No. That's for later."

"What are we doing later?"

That sexy smile appeared. "You'll see."

Yep. Big trouble. She had a million questions, but he just continued walking. They bypassed the ticket window and got in line. Apparently, he had really done some planning because he'd purchased the tickets online beforehand. They had arrived an hour early for the ten-fifteen scheduled departure and, as a result, had a position near the front of the line.

When it came time to board, Brandon asked, "Do you want to sit inside or on the top deck?"

"If there are still seats available, I'd like to sit on the top deck." Since the sun was shining and the weather not too cool, she thought it might be a better way to take in the scenery.

The ride to the island took about an hour. Faith stepped off the boat and glanced around the quaint area. Shops lined the walk all around and houses sat on hills behind them. "What are we going to do first?" she asked. "It's a beautiful day." Sun, blue skies, slight breeze and though the temperature said mid seventies, it felt at least ten degrees warmer.

Brandon shrugged. "That's up to you. We can walk around, shop, do one of the tours…"

"Let's walk for a few minutes and first, then we can decide." They passed several souvenir shops, restaurants and bike and golf cart rental places. Off to her right, Faith spotted what seemed to be a boat that looked like a submarine. She pointed. "Is that a submarine?"

"Looks like one." He led her across the planked walk and stopped at the tour window. He picked up a brochure, opened it and held it where Faith could see.

She read descriptions for the different tours. "There is a semi-submarine tour that looks interesting." She had never done anything like it. "And it's only forty-five minutes long."

Luckily, there were still a few tickets available for the eleven forty-five trip, so he bought two. "Perfect timing."

They only had to wait ten minutes before boarding, navigating down a steep flight of stairs to a narrow interior that had rows of seats on either side, each one in front of a window. The boat moved through the water while the guide gave some history and talked about the various types of fish they might see. Faith saw a variety of large and small fish, and tried to match them with the pictures posted above them on the walls.

At one point, the fish swarmed the boat when the captain stopped to feed them. She felt the same excitement as the two young children who squealed and raced from window to window. She and Brandon snapped several pictures on their phones. He even asked the person sitting across from them to take one of him and Faith. She leaned over to look at it and felt a strange sensation. Ignoring it, she said, "That's a nice one. Can you send it to me?" Brandon pushed a few buttons on his phone and a moment later, hers buzzed. Faith studied it for a minute. Brandon had his arm around her, their heads touching, and both were smiling. They weren't a real couple, but for today, she could pretend. At the end, they climbed the steps and stepped out into the sunshine again. "That was cool."

"Yeah, it was pretty cool."

Faith gazed up at him with amusement. "I take it you've never done something like this, either." She shook her head. "You need to get out of your office more."

Brandon ducked his head sheepishly. "We've already established that I don't leave the office often, but hey, I should get some points. This is the second time in as many weeks that I've taken time out to play."

She patted him on the chest. "You're absolutely right, baby." Coming up on tiptoe, she gave him a quick kiss, grabbed his hand and pulled him in the direction of the main street. "I'm hungry." They ended up at Jack's Country Kitchen, where they both ordered the Catalina Club.

Afterward, he rented a golf cart and they spent the next hour touring the island. When they got back, she had enough time before their three-thirty return to purchase a T-shirt and two bottles of nail polish that went on one color, but changed in the sunlight.

He was still shaking his head when they boarded the boat. "Nail polish?"

"What? It's like getting two colors for one price and if you want to change the color, all you do is have to step outside. You can't beat that."

Brandon laughed. "Whatever you say."

Once again, they opted to sit on the top deck. The breeze

had kicked up a little and blew her hair in her face. Brandon scooted closer to Faith and slung his arm around her. He gently turned her face toward him, pushed her hair back and placed a lingering kiss on her lips. Faith's eyes slid closed. The feel of his warm lips on hers caused a riot of sensations. She had promised herself she'd pull back, but it became harder every second they spent together. She stared out over the water and searched her mind for a reason to end the evening early.

"Did you enjoy yourself?"

"I had a wonderful time. Thank you. So, what's next?" Faith wanted to know why he'd had her bring a change of clothes. He'd told her comfortable shorts or sweats were fine, so she assumed they wouldn't be going any place that required them to dress up. And had he brought a change, as well?

"A little relaxation before dinner, and then we'll see." Brandon's eyes twinkled with amusement at the look she gave him. "Haven't I been a good host since you've been here?"

He had been a fabulous host and more. "Yes."

He kissed her temple. "Nothing's going to change tonight." He leaned closer until they were a whisper apart. "In fact, I want it to be one you remember for a long time."

"I remember every moment we've been together," Faith said, the words tumbling out before she could stop them.

Brandon traced a finger down her cheek. "So do I."

She could *not* fall for this man. He pulled her closer and they remained that way for the duration of the ride. After disembarking, they made their way back to the car. She tried to hide a yawn.

"Tired?" he asked.

"Not really. It's just something about being outside all day that totally relaxes me." In reality, she could barely keep her eyes open. Between the temperatures that had climbed into the eighties and fighting off her desire for Brandon, she needed a long nap.

"Well, you'll have time to chill before we eat."

Faith smiled, leaned back against the seat and closed her eyes. The lulling movement of the car relaxed her further and she drifted off. When she opened her eyes the next time, almost half an hour had passed. She didn't recognize the stretch of highway they were traveling on, but she did recognize the traffic that seemed to be a constant fixture since she had been in LA. She sat up and glanced over at Brandon. He sang quietly and bobbed his head in time with the up-tempo R&B song playing. As if sensing her scrutiny, he turned his head her way.

"Hey, sleepyhead."

She chuckled. "Sorry. Where are we going?"

"Brentwood. My house."

His house? "How much farther?"

"With or without traffic?"

Faith burst out laughing. "I don't know how you people deal with this all the time."

Brandon shook his head. "We should be there in about fifteen minutes."

She was admittedly curious about where he lived. He was a self-proclaimed workaholic and struck her as being a bachelor in every sense of the word. However, with the way he carried himself and dressed, she didn't think it would be the proverbial bachelor's pad. She imagined he lived in an upscale apartment or condo. He exited the freeway several minutes later. She marveled at the number of people out and about. "There are a lot of young people."

"That's because UCLA is a few miles away."

"Is that where you went to school?" She realized that he didn't talk about himself much.

Brandon left the main street and turned down a residential area. "No. I went to UC Berkeley, got an undergrad business degree and stayed for the MBA."

Faith took in the large houses and nicely manicured lawns. "I figured that's what your degree would be in." He made another turn, drove halfway down the block and pulled into the driveway of an expensive-looking two-story house. Her mouth fell open. At least she had gotten the upscale part right. He got her bag from the trunk and came around to help her out. "This is very nice." Greenery lined the front and, despite the browning from heat and drought, the grass looked freshly cut. "Somehow, I expected you to live in a condo or something."

He smiled. "Until six months ago, I did." He led her to the front door, unlocked it and moved back for her to enter.

She stepped inside a large foyer with highly polished wood floors.

"Come on in and I'll give you the grand tour."

The foyer opened to a large living room that held a sofa, love seat, two lamps and a coffee table. A trio of paintings rested against the fireplace waiting to be hung. She followed him to a chef's kitchen with an island. "Your home is gorgeous. But, why so much space since you live alone? I would think with all the hours you work, you wouldn't have time to keep up with a house."

Brandon placed her bag on one of the stools. "I did love my condo and not having to worry about maintenance. My sister and brother-in-law live in the area and, after visiting them one time, I drove around and liked the neighborhood. I figured it would be a good investment."

A future investment that most likely included a wife and children. That thought shouldn't have bothered her, but it did.

"My brothers, sisters and I all spent a lot of time at each other's homes, and it's not unusual for one or all of them to stay the night. With both my sisters now being married, my two-bedroom condo seems to have gotten smaller. And we could get a little rowdy, which my neighbors didn't appreciate," he added with a laugh.

"I can imagine." Faith had seen the photos of his family on the website and knew that, other than Brandon, only one worked for the company. After her initial search, she had Googled his other siblings and found that one brother had been a model and now owned a fitness center, and the other one played professional football. She wanted to ask which sister lived in the area—the one married to the pro football star or the one married to the inventor—but kept the question to herself. Asking would open an entire can of worms and ruin what had, so far, been another perfect date.

"Let me show you the rest of the house, then you can relax in here or out on the deck while I cook dinner."

She whirled around. "Cook? *You're* going to cook dinner?"

Brandon placed his hand over his heart. "What's that supposed to mean? Men can't cook? I think my feelings are hurt."

She bit her lip to stifle a laugh. "I'm not saying that. I just thought that we would order in since it's been a long day."

He slid an arm around her waist, drew her close and bent close to her ear. "Nope. I'm going to cook for you and then I have a special dessert for you a little later." He rained kisses along her jaw, the shell of her ear and the expanse of her neck.

"Special dessert?" she murmured, shivering from the heat of his tongue. He could keep doing what he was doing right now and it would suffice for dessert in her book.

"Special," Brandon confirmed. "But if we don't stop, the only one eating dinner tonight will be me." Yet he kept right on kissing her. At length, he straightened. "There is just something about you, Faith, that I can't resist."

Lord knew she couldn't resist him, either, but she kept that to herself, as well. They continued to tour the rest of the four-bedroom, four-bath house and, she noted that aside from the elegant dining room and his well-used office, the one downstairs and two upstairs spare bedrooms were still awaiting furniture. The master suite boasted dark, heavy furniture and had been done in varying shades of blue with gray accents. Faith noted a cozy sitting area holding two loungers and a fireplace through an archway on the other side of the room. He had a sophisticated sound system, wall-mounted television, a large, walk-in closet and luxurious spa-like bathroom. "I see you made sure to have this room furnished."

He shrugged. "Hey, I needed somewhere to sleep other than the cramped pullout sofa in my office."

Faith laughed and eyed his tall, muscular frame. "Yeah, I can see how that would be a problem."

Brandon smiled.

She started from the room and headed down the stairs.

"Here's my other sleeping spot."

She surveyed the family room. "It looks like you spend a lot of time in here." The area held a large sofa, two over-size recliners, end tables, another fireplace and a huge TV mounted on the wall.

"When I'm home, yes. But by the time I get home most nights, the only thing I want is my bed."

"Are you putting furniture in the other bedrooms?"

"Sooner or later. I want to add a few more things to the living room. I haven't decided about the bedrooms yet." Back in the kitchen, Brandon folded his arms and leaned against the counter. "My mother keeps telling me she'd be more than happy to help me decorate, but I'm afraid the rooms will be as pimped out as the ones you see in magazines or on television." He frowned and shook his head. "I like things simple. Nice, but simple."

Faith had to admit, the house suited him and there wasn't a sock out of place. "Do you have someone to come in and clean?"

He pushed off the counter, opened the sliding glass door and inclined his head. "About every four to six weeks, but I'm the only one here so it doesn't take much to keep it picked up."

The door led to a private backyard highlighted by a large covered stone patio and nice grassy area that would be perfect for relaxing or dining outdoors all year round. "Wow. I really like this."

"You can relax out here while I cook, if you want. Would you like a glass of wine?"

"I'd love some. Whatever you have that's light and sweet."

"I have a Riesling or sauvignon blanc. Which do you prefer?"

"Either is fine." She watched him go back inside and close the screen, and then walked over to the edge of the patio and leaned against the railing. She stared out over the yard and thought about how much she liked Brandon, how much she enjoyed being with him…and how she was going to tell him that she couldn't see him anymore.

Chapter 14

Brandon decided that they would eat on the patio since Faith seemed to enjoy being out there. All the time while cooking, he took peeks at her, watching her calm expression as she relaxed in one of the loungers and sipped her wine. She was only the second woman he'd brought to his home and he had been leery about inviting her. The last woman he'd invited over shortly after moving in had all but ordered furniture and wanted to rearrange his bedroom, claiming that it needed "a woman's touch." Brandon had cut short the plans he had for the evening and the only touch she got was when he held her hand to walk her out to her car and out of his life. He had immediately blocked her number and email address. His name was the only one on the deed and that meant *he*, alone, decided what did or did not go in *his* house.

He added chopped tomatoes, spinach, minced garlic and a dash of crushed red pepper to the pan containing sautéed shrimp and stirred. Brandon turned the heat down, drained the fettuccine pasta and added it, along with butter and a little lemon juice to the pan. Bending, he opened the oven door to check the French bread. His mother made the best bread and she had done a couple of loaves for him that he'd picked up yesterday on his way home. All he had to do was bake them for thirty minutes. The bread had another few minutes, so he stood in the doorway with his own glass and observed Faith as she slept. Her half-empty wineglass sat on the small table next and she had one hand resting across her stomach and the other one above her head. He imagined her in his bed, lying naked just this way.

She hadn't offered her opinion at all and respected his answer about when he'd get furniture without question. It was one more reason, on a growing list, why he liked her. And for the first time in three years, he contemplated them having a relationship beyond what they'd originally agreed upon. Brandon planned to ask her at the end of the evening and hopefully by then he would have made it hard for her to say no.

Going back to the oven, he removed the bread and placed it on a wire rack to cool. Then he went out to the patio to wake Faith. He squatted next to her and placed a soft kiss on her lips. "Wake up, beautiful. Dinner is ready."

Faith's eyes fluttered and opened. She gave him a smile that made his heart clench. "Hey." She sat up and stretched. "I guess being in the sun wiped me out more than I realized." She swung her legs over the side.

Brandon stood and pulled her to her feet. The evening temperatures had cooled some. For him it was perfect, but he reasoned it might be too chilly for her. "Do you want to eat out here or inside?"

She rubbed her arms. "I really want to eat out here. Let me get my jacket." He let her precede him into the house. "Oh, my. It smells good in here." She scanned the kitchen. "Is that homemade French bread?"

"It is, indeed…courtesy of my mom. All I had to do is bake it."

"I'm impressed." Faith grabbed her jacket from the bar stool where she'd left it and slipped it on. "Do you need me to help with anything?" He shook his head. "Well, if you show me where everything is, I can fix my own plate."

Brandon folded his arms. "What you can do is go sit at the table and I'll bring everything out." She gave him a look and he added, "Yeah, I know. I'm bossy." He kissed her. "Just for tonight, will you let me do this for you, baby? You can go back to telling me about myself tomorrow."

Faith wrapped her arms around his waist and laid her head on his chest. "Okay. Thank you." She released him and headed out to the deck. She stopped at the door and turned back. "Don't make it a habit." She held up a finger. "One night."

He laughed and watched her slip through the door, then took out plate settings and the cloth napkins his mother insisted he needed for special occasions and set the table. He returned, dished up the pasta in a serving bowl, sliced and placed the bread in a basket, got butter, parmesan cheese and the rest of the wine. Brandon loaded it all onto a tray and carried it out to the table.

"Wow, you're going all out."

"Is that a problem?" he asked, topping off their glasses and taking a seat across from her.

She hesitated briefly. "I… No. No it isn't."

Something in her eyes gave him pause, but he chalked it up to her being as unsure as he was about their growing feelings for each other. He waited until she fixed her plate before filling his own. "Do you want some cheese?" She nodded. He stood and grated some over the pasta.

Faith held up a hand. "That's good. Thanks." She buttered a piece of bread and took a bite. "Oh, my goodness," she said, moaning. "Tell your mother this is fabulous."

Brandon grinned. "I'll do that. How's the pasta?"

"It's really good." She peered into the bowl. "Just checking to see if there is any left. Since I'm letting you be bossy tonight, it's only fair that I get the leftovers. The bread, too."

He paused with his fork midair. "And what do I get?"

Faith leaned forward and rested her head in her hands. "Oh, I don't know. What do you want?"

He hardened immediately and it took everything in him to stay seated. The sultry smile and sparkling dark eyes tempted him to show her right then and there what he wanted. *Stick to the plan.* "If you keep looking at me like that, you're going to find out real quick." He would show her that and more. Later.

She didn't say anything else, but for the rest of the meal, the heat rose between them.

Afterward, he overrode her attempts to clean the kitchen. Instead they took their glasses of wine outside to the patio. Brandon set his on a small table. He removed a blanket from a deck box, sat on a lounger and coaxed Faith down onto his lap. He draped the blanket over her legs. "Comfortable?"

She snuggled closer. "Very. I wish I had something like this at home. I'd be out there every evening."

"You're welcome to come hang out anytime," he said without thought.

She angled her head and studied him as if she couldn't believe his offer.

"I mean it." Normally, the idea of any woman having free rein in his private space would send him running in the opposite direction. This time, however, he didn't feel the same panic taking hold and wondered why.

"We'll see."

They sat in companionable silence as the sun went down and the stars came out. It had been a long time since Brandon enjoyed being with a woman so much and he hoped she'd be receptive to his plan.

"Are we going anywhere else?" Faith asked sometime later.

"No, why?"

"Just wondering since you had me bring a change of clothes." She shifted in his lap and looked up at him. "Then what do I need them for?"

"For you to change into later." She narrowed her eyes and he smiled inwardly. "Are you ready for the next part of our evening?"

"What are you up to, Brandon?"

"Just trying to make sure I'm better than good." Brandon swung his legs around, stood with Faith in his arms and carried her inside and upstairs to his master bathroom. He placed her on her feet. "I have something special planned for you after your bath."

Faith placed her hands on her hips.

"You gave me one night to be bossy and I plan to take full advantage." He filled the tub and added some of the vanilla bubble bath he'd purchased.

"Why are you doing this?" she whispered. "This is... I mean we're not really..."

"I know." He understood what she meant. Technically, they weren't in a relationship and, normally, he would never go to such lengths for a woman with whom he had a very temporary arrangement. "But there's something growing between us, Faith, and I don't want it to stop."

She gasped softly.

Brandon had planned to wait until later to tell her what he was feeling, but she'd asked. "I know what I said at the beginning, what we agreed to."

"Brandon, I like you." Faith ran a hand over her forehead. "But I don't think it's going work. I'm going home in two weeks—"

He cut her off with a kiss. "We can talk about it later. Tonight I want to show you how much I *really* like you. Tonight I want it to be all about us." He lit the candles he'd placed around the tub's edge and on the sink, then gave her a set of towels. Kissing her once more, he said, "When you're done, meet me downstairs."

Faith took the towels. "Can you bring my clothes?"

He walked to the door. "You won't need them. Just the towel."

She stared. "Where are you going to be?"

Brandon turned and smiled. "You'll know." He closed the door behind him, grabbed a pair of shorts and went to take a shower in one of the other bathrooms. Tonight he was pulling out all the stops.

Faith lingered in the tub, surrounded by the soft scent of vanilla, and not knowing what to do. She had tried to tell Brandon that they needed to pull back—okay she hadn't tried too hard—but with his soft confession and the candlelit bath, she couldn't do it. She didn't want to. A woman would kill to have a man do the things Brandon had done for Faith.

She finished washing up, stood and stepped out of the tub. After drying and wrapping the towel around her, she left to find Brandon. She stopped short upon seeing a path of rose petals at the bottom of the stairs. Tentatively, she followed them down the hall and to where they stopped at the entrance to one of the empty bedrooms he had shown her earlier.

Faith pushed the door open slowly and brought both of her hands to her mouth. "Brandon, it's beautiful," she said softly, feeling tears stinging her eyes. He'd lit candles around the room, placed a massage table covered by a sheet and surrounded by rose petals in the center and had a tray off to the side with three bottles of oil and a warmer.

Brandon stood shirtless in a pair of basketball shorts. Obviously, he had showered, as well.

Brandon held his hand out to her. "Come here, sweetheart."

She crossed the room to him and cupped his jaw. "I have never met anyone like you. Thank you for this."

He turned his face and kissed the center of her palm. He stripped the towel away and gestured for her to climb up on the table face down. "Comfortable?"

"Mmm, yes." A moment later, she heard soft music and recognized Raheem DeVaughn's "Countdown To Love." A shiver passed through her when Brandon trailed a path down the center of her spine with his tongue. Next, she felt the warm oil and his hands on her shoulders and back. The combination of light, deep and feather-like touches aroused her as much as they relaxed her. He moved down her back, adding soft kisses. Faith lost all sense of time and place, and gave herself totally to the sensations. He kneaded her buttocks, slipped lower, grazed her core and continued to her inner and outer thighs, legs and feet. Her breathing deepened and her skin tingled with awareness.

Brandon had her turn onto her back and began the magic again. Throughout the entire massage, he hadn't uttered one word, but she could hear his increased breathing. He caressed and suckled her breasts, traced a path down the front of her body to her center. His fingers dipped into her center, stroking slowly. Faith moaned. He used his hands to take her to the brink of ecstasy, then bring her back to relaxation over and over until she thought she might lose her mind from all the pleasure. By the time he finished, her body pulsed and shuddered.

Brandon pulled her to a sitting position and stepped between her spread legs. "I love touching your beautiful body," he murmured as his hands continued roaming.

He slanted his mouth over hers in a deep, sensual kiss

that left her gasping for air. Faith reached inside his shorts and grasped his engorged shaft and nearly wept with relief when she realized he already had on a condom. "I need you inside me, Brandon. Now."

He yanked his shorts down and entered her with one long stroke. They both moaned. "I told you before, you don't ever have to beg me and I'll never make you wait."

Faith wrapped her legs around his waist and gripped the edge of the table as he plunged in and out of her, hitting her sensitive spot with each rhythmic push. Because of his earlier foreplay, she didn't last a minute. She screamed out his name. Brandon tilted her hips and thrust harder until she convulsed in a blinding climax that shook her entire body. She had never met a man like him and, despite her best efforts, she'd fallen for him. Completely.

Brandon held himself still while she contracted around him and he grit his teeth to maintain control. Slowly, he pulled out, placed Faith on her feet with her back to him and eased inside again. In this position, he had a full view of her flaring hips and shapely bottom and he felt himself grow harder with the sight. He bent her forward over the table and started a slow, easy rhythm, wanting to build her passions again and hear her scream his name.

"Brandon, baby," Faith panted, "don't stop."

He couldn't stop if he wanted to, not with her being so tight, so wet. She clamped down on him with her inner muscles and he cursed. "Don't do that. You're gonna make me come."

"Isn't that the point?"

She did it again and electricity shot through his body. Brandon lost it. He pounded into her harder and faster and she clenched him again and again, demanding that he give her everything. She screamed even louder and that did it for him. The orgasm began somewhere around his feet and shot through him with a force that rocked his soul. And as hard as he tried to hold back that hidden, protected part, he couldn't. He drew her down to the carpet and they both lay there trying to catch their breath.

"You were right," Faith said a few minutes later. "This was better than good."

Brandon chuckled. "Glad you approve." When he could move, he got up, blew out the candles and led her up to his bedroom, where they showered and fell into his bed. It was almost one and he had intended to take her home, but needed to sleep for an hour first.

He woke up with a start when something solid bumped him. It took a moment to remember that he wasn't in bed alone. Faith lay pressed into his side with her leg thrown over his. He yawned and glanced over at the clock. *Almost five!* His eyes widened and his stomach clenched. He had never done a morning after, not even with the woman he'd dated for two years. Mornings after implied way too much intimacy and thoughts of permanency, things he steered clear of.

Brandon carefully shifted her and sat up. He needed to think about what he wanted from this relationship. He knew he wanted to keep seeing her, but beyond that he had no idea. He stared at her sleeping so peacefully. Justin's words came back to Brandon: *There's nothing like waking up beside that one special woman every day.* He slid off the bed, scrubbed a hand down his face and paced the length of the floor. He wasn't ready for the whole one-woman-for-life thing. Or was he? He stopped pacing. A moment of panic gripped him and he took a deep breath.

"You're okay. It's just one night," he mumbled to himself. "You'll be taking her home in a few hours and everything will be back to normal." Brandon slipped back into the bed, the pressure in his chest easing. Besides, he didn't have to think about that just yet because Faith would be leaving in a couple of weeks. A different type of anxiety took hold at the thought of her going back home. Was he going crazy? He'd never had such conflicting emotions about a woman. With everything swirling around in his head, he thought it might be best if he waited to discuss any long-term plans. He had time. Brandon tried to go back to sleep, but with his mind racing, ended up staring at the ceiling.

Faith stirred and opened her eyes. "Good morning. What time is it?"

He glimpsed over his shoulder. "Six forty-five."

"I hadn't planned on spending the night," she murmured.

That made two of them. "Do you have anything planned for today?"

"I have some work to do and a conference call with a client later this morning."

"If I get you home by eight, will that be early enough?"

"Yes."

They lay quietly for a while longer, then got dressed and drove back to the hotel.

Inside her door, Faith placed a hand on Brandon's chest. "I don't know how to thank you for such a beautiful day and night. I had a wonderful time."

"It was my pleasure." The word *pleasure* conjured up vivid and sensual memories of last night. Her expression changed and she dropped her head. Brandon lifted her chin. "What is it, baby?"

"As much as I enjoy being with you, I don't think we should continue to see each other. We know this thing isn't leading anywhere and it makes no sense to…" She trailed off. "And there's something—"

"I realize you're going home soon, but you don't believe that any more than I do. We can take this relationship anywhere we want. And I want to take it as far as it goes."

Brandon cut her off when she started to protest. "Just think about it. We can talk later this week." He captured her mouth in a slow, drugging kiss, wanting to show her why it did make sense for them to continue seeing each other. He slid an arm around her waist, pulled her closer and deepened the kiss. She moaned and slipped her hands beneath his shirt and trailed them down his back. It was his turn to moan. On the brink of losing control, Brandon tore his mouth away and rested his forehead against hers, breathing harshly. He closed his eyes and tried to calm himself. He was two seconds from stripping her naked and going for one more round. "Just think about it and we can talk this week," he said again. He kissed her once more and left while he still could.

Brandon went home and cleaned up the kitchen and bedroom. As he gathered up the rose petals and candles, and stripped the sheets off the massage table, he recalled Faith's passionate cries and the heat of her surrounding him as he thrust in and out of her. He braced his hands on the table and bowed his head. There was no way he could go without seeing her.

He tried to catch up on some work he had brought home, but gave up after two hours. He thought about calling Khalil, but changed his mind. In his present state of mind, if his brother made one teasing remark, Brandon would end up being banned from his parents' house. He couldn't chance that happening because he enjoyed being around his family, and he loved his mama's cooking. Instead he went shopping, then took care of a few minor things around the house. But nothing calmed the restlessness he felt. The night was worse. He tossed and turned for hours, then fell asleep for an hour only to be awakened by a dream so erotic it made him call out Faith's name.

The next morning, Brandon dragged himself out of bed to go to work. He had been looking forward to the start of this new workweek and beginning the transition with his father. But with less than three hours of sleep, it would take a double shot of caffeine to get him going.

He made it to the office by seven and stopped in the first floor café for coffee before taking the elevator up to his floor. Most of the employees didn't start arriving until seven thirty, but he liked coming in earlier while it was still quiet to get a jump on the day.

"Good morning, Mrs. Collins," he said to his administrative assistant. Fifty-something-year-old Gladys Collins had been a fixture in the company since he was a kid and knew as much about the company as Brandon. Over the years, his father had tried offering her various management positions, but she'd turned them down each time, saying she liked her job just fine.

"Morning, Brandon. Here are your messages." Mrs. Collins handed him a small stack.

Brandon skimmed them. Most were from suppliers on the East Coast. "Thank you." He opened the door to his inner office and closed it behind him. He tossed the messages on the desk and booted up his computer and sipped his coffee. Fifteen minutes later, with the caffeine pumping through his blood, he felt revived and ready to tackle the training document he'd been working on for his replacement. He had a hard time because his thoughts kept drifting to Faith and his growing feelings.

After two hours of barely making progress, Brandon decided that he needed to talk to someone. He told his assistant he'd be back and sought out his brother-in-law. He knocked on the partially open door of the office Justin used when he came. "Hey, Justin. Got a minute?"

Justin's head came up and his fingers stilled on the keyboard of his laptop. "Hey, Brandon. Yeah, have a seat." He shifted the computer to the left of the near empty desk and clasped his hands together.

He dropped down in the chair.

"What's up?"

"How did you know Siobhan was the one?" Brandon held up a hand. "You can skip the intimate details."

A slow smile spread across Justin's face. "I didn't. I had no intentions of starting anything serious and Siobhan felt the same." He shook his head. "I can't put my finger on when or how it happened, but all of a sudden I found myself falling in love." He angled his head thoughtfully. "Is that how you're feeling about Faith?"

"I don't know. It's just different. I've never been distracted by a woman before, but I can't stop thinking about Faith."

"Is she still here?"

"Yes, but she's going back to Portland in a couple of weeks." Brandon didn't know how he was going to handle not being able to see her whenever he wanted. Any visits would have to be coordinated between their schedules and with him taking over the company, it could be a few months before his schedule cleared. That didn't sit well with him, either. "I mentioned continuing our relationship, but we haven't really had time to discuss it at length."

Justin leaned forward. "If you care about her, don't let her get away. I can't tell you how hard it was when I thought I'd lost Siobhan. Whatever you do, don't let her get away," he repeated, as if he were remembering.

Brandon nodded. Now how in the hell was he going to accomplish that?

Chapter 15

Wednesday evening, Faith fiddled with the salad on her plate as she talked to Brandon on the phone. They hadn't spoken since he dropped her off on Sunday, due to his work schedule, and she'd missed his call earlier in the day because of a conference call. He was still campaigning to convince her to continue their relationship. But she knew once she came clean, he would, more than likely, never speak to her again, much less date her.

"How did your conference call go this afternoon?" Brandon was asking.

"It went well. I may have another client, but I have to wait until I send my proposal."

"That's great news. By the way, I brought your idea of student interns to my company and got very positive responses, so thank you."

She hadn't realized he had paid that much attention to what she said. "You're welcome. I'm sure it'll turn out well."

"I've been meaning to ask if things were still going well with your father."

"Yes. We're enjoying getting to know each other." Not wanting to talk about her father, Faith changed the subject. "Have you thought more about working with your uncle's replacement?"

"No. And we're going to have to agree to disagree on the subject. Maybe we should talk about something else."

She sighed inwardly. His clipped tone gave her the impression that he was still angry and resistant to the idea, and made it that much more difficult for her to tell him. "Actually, I need to finish my dinner and get started on the proposal."

Brandon's sigh came through the line. "I didn't mean to snap at you. Can we have dinner tomorrow?"

"I'll be with my father." Faith had called Thad and asked if she could come over. She had to tell him about Brandon. Maybe he would have an idea of what she should do.

"What about lunch on Friday? There's a nice café on the first floor of the building where I work."

She tried to think of a reason she couldn't go, but outside of telling him the truth, she couldn't come up with one. "Sure. What time?"

"Is two okay? That way we can miss the lunch crowd."

"Two is good." *The fewer people around, the better.* She just hoped he didn't get any ideas about her visiting his office. He gave her the address, told her to park in the underground garage and said not to worry about the cost, that he would make sure to have it validated. They talked a moment longer, then Faith ended the call.

She looked down at her half-eaten salad and pushed the plate away, her appetite now gone. She buried her head in her hands and muttered, "What am I going to do?" If she had known they would end up this way, she would have never gone out with him past that first dinner. She got up, dumped the salad and tried to work on her proposal, but after her fourth mistake, decided to call it a night. Her mind just wasn't into work.

Thinking a warm scented bath would relax her, she headed to the bathroom, turned on the water and added two capfuls of her eucalyptus spearmint bubble bath under the stream. When the tub filled, she stripped, sank down beneath the bubbles and sighed heavily. Faith tried to shut out everything crowding her brain, but found it hard. From Thad's offer and the prospect of relocating, to what her parents would say and the impending blowup with Brandon, her thoughts were a jumbled mess. To make matters worse, she admitted to herself that she had fallen in love with Brandon and was destined for another heartbreak.

Finally accepting that the calm feeling she sought would not be happening tonight, Faith washed up and got out. She sensed the beginning of a headache and opted to go to bed rather than work on the proposal. She had a week to finish and send it off, which gave her plenty of time.

After fidgeting in bed for more than two hours, she tried listening to music, then reading. Neither worked, so she turned on the TV and surfed the channels until she found reruns of *Criminal Minds*. By the third episode, her eyes glazed over and Faith woke up the next morning to the sound of the TV.

She spent much of the day working on the proposal and content for her student program. Later in the evening, she called Thad to make sure he was home and drove over.

Thad greeted her with a hug and kiss on the cheek. "How's my girl?"

"I don't know. There's a lot going on."

His brows knit. "Well, let's go talk about it." As she followed him to the family room, he asked, "Does this mean you've been thinking more about coming to work at Grays?"

Faith dropped down on the sofa and leaned her head back. "Yes, but I'm still not sure it'll be a good idea."

"Oh."

The disappointment filling his voice made her sit up. "Believe me, I thought about it, but I found out something else that is weighing heavily on my decision."

Thad leaned forward. "You're okay, right? Is your mom sick?"

"Yes, and no. That's not it." She tried to figure out where to start and decided on the beginning. "The day after I arrived in LA on my first visit, I was in a car accident."

He gasped. "Were you hurt? Why didn't you call me?"

Faith smiled faintly. *Once a parent, always a parent.* "It was kind of freaky." She shared the details of what happened, why she had been on the freeway and why she didn't call.

"I wish you had called me, Faith. It wouldn't have mattered that you were just showing up after so long. You're my daughter and I would have gladly taken care of you."

"I know that now, but a really nice guy stopped to see if I was all right, stayed with me until the ambulance arrived and brought my stuff to the hospital." She paused. "And I've been seeing him since."

Thad's eyes lit up. "Is he a nice young man?"

Brandon's smile flashed in her head, along with every moment they had spent together since she woke up in the hospital and saw him sitting in the chair. "He's very nice."

He shook his head in confusion. "I'd think it'd be easier to make the decision to move if he's such a nice fellow." He raised a brow. "Unless he's not as nice as you say."

Faith chuckled. "No, he really is a nice guy." Her smile faded. "But I found out when I checked out the Gray Home Safety website—like you asked—that he's the same man who's going to assume the CEO position."

Surprise filled his face. "Brandon? You've been dating Brandon since you got here?"

"Yes."

Thad laughed. "That's wonderful. Since you two know each other already and get along well, it'll be easy to work together."

She shook her head slowly. "Brandon was frustrated about the delay in him assuming the leadership role and told me about 'Uncle Thad's mystery child' and he was not happy. Apparently, he anticipated running the company alone and wants to keep it that way."

"That boy has always been intense, but he usually comes around."

"I don't think so...not this time." She thought back on the disagreement that led to her asking him to leave and their conversation yesterday and didn't see him changing his stance anytime soon, if ever. "Because I know how he feels, there's no way I can take that position now."

"That VP position belongs to you just as much as the CEO position does to him. He knows how important family legacy is. Don't let him cheat you out of your inheritance. I'll have a talk with Nolan. He'll—"

"No, no. Please don't."

Thad studied her. "You haven't told him."

"No," she answered softly. "I tried a couple of times, but we kept getting interrupted." An image of Brandon's hands trailing over her body and making love to her on the massage table appeared in her mind. Her nipples tightened and her core pulsed. Faith quickly pushed the vision aside. "But I plan to tell him tomorrow, so please don't say anything."

"I won't, but you remember I want to introduce you next Tuesday."

"I do." She definitely had to tell him before then. He'd

hate her even more if she walked through that door and he found out she knew beforehand.

He patted her hand. "I know you're worried, but don't be. Everything will work out. Now I'd be lying if I said I wasn't happy about the two of you getting together. However, now that Brandon is dating my baby girl, that changes his position. I love him like a son, but I'll roast him on a spit if he breaks your heart."

Faith almost laughed, but the serious expression on Thad's face stopped her. She realized he meant every word and the fact that he hadn't seen her in twenty-eight years meant nothing. He was still her father and he took that to heart. She wanted to tell him that he might as well dig the pit and start the fire because her heart was already breaking.

Friday, Brandon spent the first part of the morning meeting with his father and now sat going through the stack of applications and resumes for his replacement. He had wanted to keep it in-house, but his father wanted to make sure they had an adequate pool of candidates and released the announcement to the general public. So far, there were nine candidates and only four were current employees of Grays. He picked up the next folder, opened it and groaned.

"Seriously?" he muttered. Why in the world had Gordon Samuels applied for the position? The man had worked here for fifteen years in the PR department and believed they should continue doing business the same way as they did when he started, regardless of the changes in technology. That was one reason he did not get the promotion to PR director and Siobhan did. The other being he always looked just short of rumpled. Needless to say, he would not be leading the home safety division, either. Brandon closed the folder, tossed it aside and opened the next one.

He had just picked up a résumé when his cell buzzed. He slid it in front of him, swiped the screen and read the message from Faith: I'm downstairs. He closed the folder, pushed to his feet and hurried to the elevator.

While riding the elevator down, Brandon mentally rehearsed what he would say. Parts of him wanted to tell her how much she had come to mean to him, that he was falling in love with her. He had wrestled with his emotions and finally accepted it, but Faith still seemed reluctant and he didn't want to scare her off. When they'd first met, she'd told him he was very direct, and usually he was. The elevator doors opened and he stepped around the people waiting to board and spotted Faith standing by the entrance to the café. She had on a sleeveless top and a slim skirt that stopped a few inches above her knees and revealed her shapely legs—the same legs that were wrapped tightly around him Saturday night as they shared the most intense pleasure. He smiled. No, this time he needed a gentler approach.

"Hey, Faith." Brandon came up behind her and placed a kiss on her cheek.

Faith whirled around. "Brandon. Hey."

He took her hand and started for the café entrance, then stopped. "Wait. Let me take care of the parking validation first, so I don't forget." He held out his hand. "Do you have it with you?"

"Yes." She removed it from her purse and handed it to him.

He took it over to the information desk for the receptionist to stamp it, came back and gave it to Faith, then escorted her into the restaurant. As he suspected, the lunch rush had passed and it only took them a minute to be seated and give their orders.

"This is nice," Faith said.

"And the food is good. Before the new owner took over, the only thing I came in for was coffee."

She laughed. "That bad, huh?"

Brandon loved her laugh. It always did something to him. "That bad."

"How long has the new owner been here?"

"Somewhere close to two years, I think." They continued to make small talk until the food arrived.

Faith picked up her grilled chicken sandwich. "Okay, let's see how good this is."

He watched as she took a bite of the selection he had suggested and chewed. He smiled when her eyes lit up and she groaned. "Told you."

"Most times the chicken breast is dry and tastes like somebody forgot the salt. But this one is juicy and seasoned perfectly."

Brandon bit into his own chicken sandwich. For a few minutes they ate in silence. "Are things still going well with your father?"

"Yes. I'll miss him when I leave, but I told him I'd be back later in the year. He's also said he'll visit me."

The fact that she would be back gave him hope their relationship could grow. "I'm sure he's happy about that." Silence rose between them as they continued to eat. When she finished, he asked, "Do you like LA?"

She took a sip of her water. "Yes. Aside from all this traffic," she added with a smile.

He laughed. "Yeah, well, can't argue with you there. Besides that, do you like it well enough to consider staying?"

"I can't stay," she said quietly with something like regret in her eyes.

He reached across the table for her hand. "Why not? You said that you could do your job anywhere as long as you had a laptop."

"Brandon, we agreed to see each other until I leave. And

I am leaving. I'll never forget what we shared, but there's no use in continuing something that won't last. You and I both know that this is only physical."

"You don't believe that any more than I do," Brandon said with irritation. Her eyebrow lifted. He drew in a calming breath and reminded himself he was supposed to be using a softer approach. "What I'm trying to say is that I realize what we shared started out as nothing more than physical attraction, but it's become more. And we both know it."

Faith withdrew her hand and shook her head. "It'll never work, Brandon."

"It will, if we want it to. And I do. You can't tell me you don't feel what's happening between us." For a moment, she said nothing and he wondered if he had been wrong—that she didn't feel the same way. She stared at him for what seemed like forever before answering.

"I do."

He reached for her hand again. "We're good together, and I'm not just talking about in the bedroom. Neither of us expected this, but I know we can make it work."

"It won't. The first time I don't agree with you we'll have another episode like last week and I don't want to have to spend time worrying whether what I say is going to set you off."

It was all Brandon could do to curb the smart-aleck response poised on the tip of his tongue. What he started to say would guarantee an argument and prove her point. He'd been working hard to tone it down, both personally and professionally and at this point, it was turning out to be one of the most difficult undertakings of his life. "I've readily acknowledged that shortcoming, but I also promised to work on it and I am."

She regarded him silently for a moment. "I believe you, Brandon. But there's something I—"

His cell phone rang. "It's probably my assistant. Let

me get this." He let go of her hand, fished it out of his pocket and answered without looking at the display. "This is Brandon."

"Where are you?" Morgan asked. "Some people have jobs and can't spend all day waiting for you, so get your butt up here, Mr. CEO."

Brandon groaned. He had completely forgotten about the meeting they'd scheduled to discuss the retirement party. "I'll be there in a minute." He hung up and pocketed the phone. He really didn't want to leave right now, especially with nothing resolved between him and Faith. "I have to go. I forgot I had a meeting." A thought occurred to him. It would be a good time to introduce Faith, since all of his siblings were here. And it would show her that he was serious about them.

"No problem."

"Would you like to meet my brothers and sisters? They're all here so we can discuss my dad's retirement."

"No," Faith answered, a little too quickly.

Something—he didn't know what—flashed in her expression.

"You're already late and shouldn't keep them waiting." She waved him on. "Go ahead. I can take care of the bill this time."

Brandon ignored her, pulled out his wallet and placed some bills on the table. "You already know my answer to that." He slid out of the booth and came around to her side. "We'll continue this conversation tonight." He bent and kissed her. "You said I was direct, but I can also be persuasive. So here's a little warning, sweetheart." He leaned down close to her ear. "I *will* be taking my A-game to the next level." Brandon smiled at her stunned expression, then sauntered out of the café, confident she would be his. He had never been one to back down from a challenge, even an unspoken one. And he wouldn't start now.

Chapter 16

Friday evening, Faith chewed nervously on her bottom lip while waiting for Brandon to arrive. Their lunch date hadn't gone anywhere near how she had planned and she regretted not having the chance to tell him the truth. Though he'd mentioned working on not flying off the handle, she couldn't help but speculate on whether he'd be able to keep that promise. In a perfect world, he would listen to everything she said, they'd discuss it like two mature adults, and he would respond calmly and rationally. But the world wasn't perfect. He had said they were good together and she hoped that *goodness* extended to the boardroom.

Faith glanced at her watch. *6:27 p.m.* She desperately needed to talk to someone and took a chance that Kathi had made it home from work. She grabbed her cell and called.

"Hey, Faith," Kathi answered.

She sighed with relief. "Hey, girl. I need some advice."

"What's wrong?"

"Everything." She and Kathi hadn't spoken since Faith

had told her about Thad's offer. Faith spent a few minutes telling her about the blowup with Brandon and what she'd found out when she went to the Gray Home Safety website. "And with how angry Brandon got the last time, I don't know how to tell him."

"It sounds like you guys have gotten closer and get along great, so I don't see why he would have a problem."

Faith told herself the same thing, but didn't believe it would work out that way. "We had lunch today and he wants us to continue seeing each other after I go home. Actually…he suggested I stay in LA."

"Wait. *What?* Hold up, girl. I think you've been holding out on me. No man is going to ask you to move there unless he's thinking about something permanent." There was a pause, and then Kathi screamed. "Oh, my God, are you in *love* with him?"

Faith flopped back against the sofa and closed her eyes. "It wasn't supposed to happen this way." She groaned. "I don't know what I was thinking."

Kathi laughed. "You weren't thinking. You were *feeling*. I know how that is. I end up saying those three little words and agreeing to a whole lot of stuff when Cameron gets me going."

"You're not helping, Kat." Though she was right.

"Does he know?"

"Of course not! And I won't be telling him because it doesn't matter."

"I disagree. If he's asking you to move there, I can't see him being mad about working with you everyday. You'd be right where he wants you."

"If only things were that simple." Admittedly, Faith expected that she and Brandon would work well together. And because she knew nothing about home safety, she had no problems letting him have the final say on any issues that might come up. But she was fairly certain he wouldn't sit still long enough for her to communicate that to him. "Thanks for letting me vent. Brandon will be here any time, so…" Her cell beeped with another call. She took a quick peek at the display. "Kathi, Thad is calling on the other line."

"Go talk to him. Keep me posted and I hope things work out for you and Brandon."

"Thanks." Faith ended the call and clicked over. "Hi, Thad."

"Hey, Faith. I wanted to see how you're doing and find out if you've had a chance to talk to Brandon."

"I'm okay and no. He's on his way over, so I'll tell him then. I tried to tell him earlier, but he had to leave for a meeting." Brandon had invited her to meet his siblings and the only thing on her mind had been running into Thad. If Thad had seen her, no way would he have pretended not to know Faith. She was glad he or someone from Brandon's family hadn't come down to the café. "I don't think it's going to go very well."

"I wouldn't worry too much. Brandon understands the importance of family legacy. Besides, if you two have grown as close as I think, he'll be happy to have you near. I know I would," Thad said with a little laugh. "Nothing wrong with having a pretty girl around every day."

She rolled her eyes and chuckled. "Yeah, I bet."

"Well, you don't have too much time because the meeting is on Tuesday."

Faith sighed heavily. "I know. Is this a board of directors meeting?"

"There isn't a formal board of directors. Since we don't have investors or shareholders, we have more of what would be described as an advisory committee and we typically meet three to four times a year. Aside from me, Nolan and his five children, there are four experts in the field of home safety who give input on trends, risk management and other things."

"I see. Will they all be there on Tuesday?"

"Yes. I suspect DeAnna, as well as Siobhan and Morgan's husbands will be there, too."

"That's a lot of people." She recognized Brandon's mother's and sister's names and remembered Thad mentioning the two sisters were married. This was getting worse by the minute. Families tended to stick together on an issue and if Brandon didn't agree with Faith being there, chances were his siblings and parents wouldn't, either.

"Faith, I know you're a little nervous, but everything will work out fine. I've known Nolan and DeAnna for over thirty-five years and they're good people. As I told you before, both are anxious to see you again."

"What about Brandon's siblings?"

"They'll welcome you with open arms."

She wished she shared his optimism. She opened her mouth to ask him another question and heard a knock at the door. Brandon. "Thad, I think Brandon's at the door."

"Okay. Let me know how it goes. If you need me, call me."

"I will."

"I love you, Faith, and will always be here for you. Never forget that."

"I won't." How could she? Most men would have given up searching for and hoping to reconnect with their child after a few years, but not Thad. She said goodbye and went to answer the door.

"Hey, beautiful," Brandon said, smiling as he entered.

"Hi." The man seemed more irresistible each time she saw him and Faith couldn't decide which attire she liked seeing him in more—the tailored slacks and dress shirt or a T-shirt and shorts. He had obviously come from work because he had on the former. Once they were settled on the sofa, butterflies took flight in Faith's stomach.

Brandon scooped her up and placed her on his lap. "Do you know how hard it was for me to sit across from you today and not kiss you like I wanted?"

He didn't give Faith a chance to answer before his mouth came crashing down on hers, hot and demanding. His tongue swirled around hers, while his hand slid up her bare thigh, heating her all over. He shifted her so she was straddling him and continued to devour her mouth. Any coherent thoughts she might have had dissolved with each tantalizing stroke. She didn't know how, but she found the strength to pull away. "Brandon, we need to talk."

"We are talking, baby." His hands slid over her hips and back, and then came up to frame her face. Their eyes met. "Don't you hear what I'm saying?" He stripped her shirt off.

Faith's pulse spiked. "This isn't…ooh…talking." She shivered in response to the slow, meandering kisses on the tops of her breasts.

"I beg to differ. Listen closely to what I'm saying," he murmured, divesting her of the bra and circling his tongue around her hardened nipples. "Can you hear me now?"

She cried out at the exquisite torture. Surely he didn't expect her to answer. And the only things she could hear were her labored breathing and her heart pounding in her ears.

"I'm telling you what I feel." Brandon lifted his head and kissed her again, this time softly, tenderly.

Tears stung the backs of her eyes. Yes, she heard him. She *felt* him. *Loved* him.

"Let me show you, Faith. I want to show you how much you mean to me." Brandon came to his feet, still holding her in his arms and strode down across the room to her bedroom.

Faith should have protested, should have said some-thing, but she wanted this last night with him.

Brandon stared down at Faith sleeping beside him and a riot of emotions swirled around in his chest. No matter how hard he tried to tell himself otherwise—that it was just fun and great sex—his heart said something different. *I love her.* And she'd be leaving unless he could convince her to stay. He had planned to continue their conversation from lunch when he arrived, but one kiss was all it took for him to lose focus. Or redirect it. He could still feel her hands and mouth on his body and would swear he heard her whisper, "I love you," as she drifted off. It gave him hope they were on the same page.

As much as he wanted to spend the night, he had the standing appointment with his brothers at the gym in the morning and he'd never make it if he stayed. But she was sleeping so peacefully he didn't want to wake her. Bran-don left the bed silently and dressed. He used the pen and notepad provided by the hotel to write a note letting her know he would be back tomorrow afternoon to talk and placed it on the pillow next to her. He gently pushed the hair off her face and kissed her lightly. "Sleep well, baby," he whispered and slipped out quietly.

Brandon managed to get a few hours of sleep and, by the time he got to the gym, everyone else had arrived.

"I thought I was going to have to take your place," Khalil said.

Malcolm laughed and eyed Brandon critically. "By the looks of big brother, that might be a good idea. Were you working late last night again, Brandon?"

Justin and Omar threw Brandon a knowing look, but didn't comment.

Brandon bent to tighten his shoelaces. "No."

Khalil let out a short bark of laughter. "No?" He sidled

next to Malcolm and elbowed him playfully. "I think Brandon is going to be playing on the other team soon," he said, gesturing toward Justin and Omar.

Malcolm's eyes widened and he whipped his head around toward Brandon. "You're dating someone seriously? Who is she?"

Brandon knew he'd have to deal with his brothers sooner or later. "None of your business." He picked up the ball. "Are we playing or not?"

Instead of playing a full game, they opted for a shoot-around. During the game, the conversation went from the current state of politics to sports and everything in between.

"Brandon, do you know what this meeting is about on Tuesday?" Khalil asked as he made a shot.

"I'm guessing it has to do with Uncle Thad's *heir*." He still got heated every time he thought about it.

Malcolm tossed Omar the ball. "Do you know anything about him?"

"I can't get Dad to tell me anything." He launched the ball and sank a three-point shot. "It's bugging the hell out of me. All I keep thinking is this guy is going to come in and try to take over."

"As CEO, you'll still have the last word, so he can't really take over," Justin offered.

Brandon divided a look between his brothers-in-law. "Are you two going to be there?"

Both nodded and Omar said, "Morgan asked me to be there, and whatever my baby wants, she gets. And I agree with Justin. You're just going to have to learn how to be a team player."

Malcolm burst out laughing. "Now *that* I'd like to see. Brandon has always run solo in everything, even when he wasn't the boss. Khalil, remember when he worked inventory back in high school that summer?"

"Yeah. Somehow, he had everyone playing to his tune, the supervisor included. And growing up, whenever we played a game, he had to be the one who set the rules."

Brandon glared. "Are you two done?" Listening to them brought back the argument he'd had with Faith. She had said some of the same things.

"Are we lying?" Malcolm asked.

No, they weren't, but that wasn't the point. And he didn't have to justify his actions to them. Both of his brothers had chosen careers outside of the company and had no interest in working there now or in the future, so they couldn't understand how hard Brandon had worked to prove himself to their father.

"Guess that's a no," Khalil said. "Enough of that. I want to go back to this mystery woman. If it's serious, why haven't you introduced her?"

"I never said it was serious. You did." He had wanted her to meet his family yesterday and she'd quickly turned him down. He was still puzzled by her response.

Omar passed the ball to Justin and said to Brandon, "I'm assuming this is the same woman from the accident."

"Yeah."

"A word of advice, my brother. If she's got you tied up like this, she might the *one*. Don't let her get away."

"Duly noted, Drummond."

They played for another hour, then called it a day. Malcolm and Khalil had other plans, but Brandon joined Omar and Justin for lunch at Omar's parents' restaurant, Miriam's Place, named after his mother.

Once they were settled and the server had taken their order, Justin said, "So, you're in love with Faith."

Brandon didn't know how to answer. Love was never an emotion he could rightfully say ever played a part in his past relationships. Lust, yes, but never love. But what he felt for Faith went well beyond just the physical. "I think so."

Omar chuckled. "You think so? If you plan to stake your claim on this woman, you'd better *know* if you are."

He leaned back in his chair and ran a hand over his head. "Yeah, I am."

Justin folded his arms. "Does she know?"

He thought back to last night when they were making love. He'd told her several things about how he felt, but fear had kept him from uttering those three little words. "I didn't actually say those words, but…" He trailed off when both Omar and Justin laughed. "What?"

Justin leaned forward and braced his clasped hands on the table. "Brandon, if you love her, you need to tell her."

"And not just beat around the bush," Omar added. "Don't be afraid to say those magic words. She needs to know you're serious."

Brandon considered their advice. Both seemed to be very happy with their wives. In fact, he couldn't recall a time when either man wasn't smiling.

"Do you plan to see her sometime soon? I assume it's Faith, the woman from the accident."

"Yes, it's Faith, and I'm going over to her hotel after I leave here."

The server returned with their meals and Justin said with a knowing smile, "You can always take that to go."

He thought about it briefly and decided to wait. "There's no rush. I mean since the food is here." He recited a short blessing and picked up his fork. Besides, he needed a little more time to work up the courage to be able to get those words out. It would be the first time he said them to a woman and he prayed it didn't backfire.

Chapter 17

Faith woke up Saturday morning alone in bed. She sat up, bleary-eyed, and listened for sounds of Brandon moving around, but heard nothing. She flopped back down on the pillow, covered her face and groaned. "Great. He's gone." He'd had her so out of control with passion last night they'd never got a chance to talk. She tossed the sheet aside and spotted a sheet of paper flutter off the other side of the bed. Rising, she walked over, picked it up and read:

> *Good morning, sweetheart,*
> *You were sleeping so soundly last night that I didn't have the heart to wake you. I'll be back later this afternoon to finish our conversation. And, yeah, I know we actually need to talk.*
> *Brandon*

She sat on the bed and released a deep sigh. Last night he had made love to her with a tenderness that had touched her soul and whispered endearments that made her almost believe he loved her. And, somehow, Brandon had gotten her to consent to continuing their relationship. For the first time in a long while, Faith had a man who made her happy and she could honestly see the two of them being together for a long time. What if she didn't tell him? Maybe... No. She couldn't let him walk in to that meeting on Tuesday and be blindsided. It wouldn't be fair and he'd hate her even more.

Faith tossed the note on the nightstand and went to shower. After dressing and forcing down a piece of toast and tea, she tried to do some work, but couldn't concentrate so she turned on the television and flipped through the channels. She settled on an old episode of *Law & Order*. Halfway through the show, her mind started to wander again and she shut it off. Reading didn't hold any appeal, either, so she decided a walk might help.

She put on her tennis shoes and started toward the front of the property. Since it was almost noon, she saw several people with luggage headed for the lobby to check out. Faith walked down Sepulveda Boulevard a short distance, turned and retraced her steps to the hotel. She cut through the lobby and went out to the back, where she passed a tennis court, pool and hot tub. A few people lounged next to the pool, taking advantage of the near eighty-degree weather. A fire pit surrounded by padded chairs sat in a gated area just on the other side.

Faith took a seat in one of the chairs and listened to the sounds around her—the thwack of a tennis ball being hit, water splashing in the pool, the traffic going by and the roar of an airplane engine above her. While sitting, she realized she hadn't spoken to her parents or told them about Thad's offer and pulled out her phone to call them. "Hey, Mom," she said when her mother answered.

"Faith. How are you?"

"I'm okay. How are you and Daddy doing?"

"Oh, we're good. He's taking me out on a date tonight," she added with a giggle.

Faith smiled. From the first moment William Alexander came into their lives, he had been an example of what a good husband should be. "That's great. Where are you going?"

"I have no idea. William said it's a surprise. I told him we're too old for this kind of thing."

"That is so romantic. And, Mom, you're never too old for a surprise date." A vision of her last date with Brandon floated through her mind—the cruise, dinner, the rose petals leading to a candlelit room with a massage table, his strong hands relaxing and arousing her all at the same time—

"Faith!"

Her mother's voice jolted her back to the conversation. "Huh? I'm sorry, what did you say, Mom?"

"Are you all right? I called you twice and asked when you were coming home."

"I'm fine. I'll probably be coming home in a week or so." If things went badly with Brandon, Faith might leave as soon as that Tuesday meeting was over.

"Honey, what's going on?"

How does she always know when something is bothering me? "Thad is retiring and wants me to assume the role of VP of the company where he works."

"Excuse me?"

Faith told her mother about the company Thad and his friend had started and the pact they had made regarding the home safety company. "He also wants me to take his seat on the advisory committee. He said it was my inheritance."

"I guess he did well for himself after leaving the military. But it's not…" Her mother trailed off.

"It's not what, Mom?"

"Nothing. I've interfered enough where Thad is concerned. You're an adult, so it'll be your decision. Are you going to take it? You'll certainly be set in your career."

"I don't know anything about home safety and I already have a career."

"Girl, please. You graduated from high school with a 4.3 grade point average, and college with a 4.0. Don't tell me you couldn't learn everything you needed to know. What's the real reason you're hesitating? I'm not trying to push you to take it because that would mean you moving away, but there has to be more than just you don't know anything about the business."

Faith really didn't want to go into detail about her reasons, mainly because she had never mentioned Brandon, either. The temperatures rose and the sun beat down on her. She got up and moved to another chair that was partially in the shade.

"Well?"

"Remember when I had the accident and I told you about the guy who stopped to help me?"

"The one who brought your things to the hospital?"

"Yes. Brandon and I have been seeing each other since then. I just found out that his father is Thad's best friend."

"Nolan?" she asked incredulously.

"Exactly. Because no one knew about me outside of him and his wife, Brandon always thought he would run the company alone. And he wants it that way." She explained the relationship Thad had with the Gray family.

"I'm guessing that he's not too happy learning that he's going to have you as a second-in-command."

"That's technically correct. Except he doesn't know it's me. Just that his 'Uncle Thad' has a kid who has come out of nowhere to take what Brandon considered his."

"Oh, Lord. What a mess."

What a mess was right. This little trip had turned out

to be far messier than she could have ever imagined. And she suspected it would get worse before it was all said and done.

"Are you going to tell Brandon?"

"I have to. Thad wants to introduce me to the advisory board on Tuesday. Brandon and all of his siblings will be there and I don't think it's fair to let him find out that way."

"You're right, baby, but what a choice. You know you can call if you need me. Although, I suspect Thad will take care of it. He knows, doesn't he?"

"He does." Faith recalled what Thad said he would do to Brandon if Brandon broke her heart. She had no doubt he'd make good on that threat. Over the past several weeks of getting to know Thad, he'd proven to be every bit of the father she knew he would have been had they not been separated. "I'll let you know what happens." She was starting to perspire and fanned herself with her hand.

"Okay. I love you, sweetheart, and I hope all goes well."

"I love you too, Mom. And thanks." She ended the call. Even though they didn't see eye to eye on everything, Faith was glad to have Francis Alexander as a mother and felt a little better now.

She rose, went back to her room and took a cool shower. When she came out, she noticed a text from Brandon telling her he would be over at three. That gave her two hours.

When Faith opened the door to Brandon, his heart rate sped up. She had on a tank top with thin straps and shorts, and the sight of her smooth, bare dark chocolate skin enticed him so much that he had to shove his hands in his pants pocket to keep from reaching for her. They needed to talk first. "Hey, baby." He kissed her.

"Hi." Faith opened the door wider so he could come in.

He followed her over to the sofa, sat and took her hand. "How're you doing today? I realized after I got home that

I didn't really play fair when it came to you agreeing to us continuing our relationship. I need to make sure that you're still okay with it."

"You didn't force me to say anything I didn't want to say, Brandon."

He smiled. "So, that means we're official." She lowered her head and his smile faded. "Faith?"

"I need to tell you something."

The serious expression on her face caused his gut to churn. She had just said they were on the same page. Or had she? "What's wrong? Did you change your mind?" She didn't speak for several long moments and his heart leaped into his throat.

"Maybe I can show you better than I can tell you." She stood, went into the bedroom and came back with a box. Faith handed him an envelope.

Brandon saw Faith's name on it and stared at her quizzically.

"Read it."

"But it's addressed to you."

"I know."

He withdrew the sheet of paper and read. It was a letter from her father saying he loved her and never stopped looking for her. His heart nearly stopped when he got to the bottom and saw the name and address. He didn't know what he expected her to tell him, but this... Brandon sat stunned for a minute, and then picked up the letter again. The wording hadn't changed. His uncle's name, address and phone number had been written in the familiar handwriting he would recognize anywhere. "Are you telling me that *you're* Uncle Thad's daughter? The one who is supposed to take his position as VP?"

Faith nodded.

Brandon jumped to his feet and paced, trying to process this news. He stopped. "So you've known all this time."

"No. I found out—"

He cut her off. "How long have you known? When she didn't respond, he gritted out, *"How long?"*

She wrapped her arms around her middle and said quietly, "Almost two weeks."

"And you didn't think this was something you should tell me?" His anger was rising by the second.

"I tried to tell yesterday at lunch, but you had to leave. Then, I tried again last night, but we got a little sidetracked."

He snorted. "You should have tried harder." Now he knew why she had declined meeting his siblings so quickly yesterday.

She glared up at him. "Obviously, you need to have your memory checked. You didn't give me time to say anything."

Brandon had to concede her that point. Last night, making love to her had been the only thing on his mind. But now he wished he had taken the time.

"And when I woke up this morning, you were gone. Besides, I knew how you would react," Faith added with a roll of her eyes.

Just like she hadn't given him a pass, he wasn't giving her one, either, with these excuses. "If you had told me before now, I wouldn't be reacting this way," he bit off tersely.

"Seriously, Brandon?" she asked incredulously. "Do you remember what you said the first time you told me about this guy coming in off the street and not knowing anything about *your company*? And then last week on the phone I asked you whether you'd changed your mind. Do you remember what you said?" Faith hopped up off the sofa and got in his face. "In case you've forgotten, let me refresh your memory."

"I don't need you to refresh my memory. My memory is just fine."

"Hmph. Well, that's something. And since you have this great recollection of what went down, then you should understand why it was hard for me to tell you. You had already decided that you hated a person you'd never met who you *thought* was going to take something from you." Her eyes flashed and her chest heaved with anger. "Here's a newsflash. I don't want to take anything from you. My father asked me to assume *his* role, not *yours*!"

Brandon leaned down close to her face. "It doesn't matter. It's still mine." He was done. She just didn't get it. And he couldn't be with a woman who was hell-bent on stealing his inheritance. "I don't think this is going to work."

"I absolutely agree. I refuse to be with a man who is stubborn, pigheaded and doesn't listen." Faith marched over to the door and snatched it open. "Get out."

Brandon stormed past her without a backward glance. She slammed the door behind him. Somewhere deep inside, his heart said he should stay, but his anger overrode all and he ignored it.

He got in his car and sped out of the lot. He engaged the Bluetooth and called Khalil.

"Hey, bro," Khalil said when he answered.

"Are you at the gym?"

"No. I'm at home. Why?"

"I'm coming over."

There was a pause in the line. "I thought you were going over to see your woman."

Brandon no longer had *a woman*. He didn't respond to Khalil's statement, but asked, "Are you going to be there for a while?"

"Yeah. Come on by."

He cut the connection. He still couldn't believe that Faith was Uncle Thad's daughter. Or that she'd kept it from Brandon. As he merged onto the freeway, it occurred to him that it might have been better if he'd gone with his first thought and dropped her stuff off at the hospital that first night and kept it moving. Now he had to find a way to get over her. To stop loving her.

Chapter 18

"He wouldn't listen to anything I said about not wanting his job," Faith cried. She'd called Kathi as soon as Brandon left. "And he didn't even acknowledge the fact that he'd been adamant about not wanting to have another person in the leadership role."

"It doesn't matter what he wants. That job and board position is rightfully yours." Kathi sighed. "I know you're trying to keep the peace, Faith, but you shouldn't have to give up your inheritance because he can't play nice with the other kids."

"It doesn't matter, anyway. I have my own business to worry about and, like I told you before, I don't know a thing about home safety."

"And like I said before, you're good at multitasking. Why can't you do both?"

"Because…because it would mean seeing Brandon everyday and I can't go through that."

"Because you love him."

"Yes." It would be too hard to have to sit next to him in meetings, remembering what they'd shared and knowing how much he despised her for being there. No, it was time for her to go home. She'd go to the meeting on Tuesday, then make plans to leave by the end of the week. Her heart was breaking and it would be best to get back to her life in Portland.

Tuesday morning, Faith sat on a bar stool in Thad's kitchen. He had called last night and invited her to stay over. He held her while she cried without saying anything, as if knowing she needed the comfort of his arms.

Thad came to where she sat and handed her a cup of green tea. "How are you feeling this morning?"

She shrugged. "Same." But she was happy that he had received his new prosthesis. He seemed to walk taller and more confidently.

He wrapped an arm around her shoulder. "Things seem a little uncertain and you're hurting right now, but everything will work out. You'll see."

"I hope so. Um… I'm going home on Friday."

He nodded his understanding.

She saw the sadness in his eyes and grasped his hand. "I promise I'll be back to visit and I'd love for you to come to Portland."

He smiled. "Nothing could keep me from visiting my baby girl."

She hadn't told him about the decisions she'd come to regarding both positions and thought this would be a good time. "I wanted to let you know that I'm not going to take the job as VP, but I will sit on the board."

"I'm disappointed, but I understand. I hope you don't mind, but I filled Nolan in on what's going on. We both agree that the job will always be yours whether you fill it now or sometime in the future." He gave her a strong hug.

The tears started again. "Thanks, Dad."

Thad went still. "That's the first time I've been called Dad since you were two," he whispered emotionally.

Faith hadn't realized she had called him Dad. The word had just slipped out, but that's who he had become to her. "You *are* my dad and I'm so glad to have you in my life again." They shared another moving hug that seemed to erase all the years they had been apart.

Thad placed a fatherly kiss on her forehead and smiled. "I tell you what, after the meeting, how about you and me going to get some ice cream. That always makes me feel better."

Faith laughed around her tears. "Only if it's two scoops of chocolate chip."

His smile widened. "That's my favorite, too."

Faith returned his smile. At least one thing had gone right in her life. For now, she turned her focus to the upcoming meeting. She still had concerns about how the rest of Brandon's family would treat her. Her father had assured her that she needn't worry, but she couldn't be sure. Family bonds were strong, and the way Brandon talked about his made her believe that their bond was stronger than most. She took a deep breath. *I just need to get through the next two hours.*

An hour later, they exited the elevator on the floor housing the company's executive offices. A sign in large black elegant lettering read "Gray Home Safety" on the wall behind a huge desk in the reception area. The woman seated there greeted them with a smile, which they returned.

Thad reached for her hand and gave it a squeeze. "Ready, baby girl?"

Faith drew in a calming breath. "As ready as I'll ever be."

Brandon sat in the conference room waiting for the meeting to start. All of his siblings were there, as well as his two brothers-in-law. He could hear bits and pieces of their conversations, speculating on Uncle Thad's child. But he knew all about her, more than he cared to at this point, but he hadn't shared the details about his relationship with Faith with anyone except Khalil. He was still angry that she hadn't told him. And even angrier that he couldn't stop thinking about her.

Khalil leaned over. "If that scowl gets any deeper, you'll have a permanent road map on your face. And I don't know why you're so mad. It's her legacy, just like the CEO is yours."

He turned a lethal glare on his brother. "There are a lot of empty chairs in here. Pick one and get the hell away from me."

He chuckled. "I'm quite comfortable where I am. And you can dial down the death glare. It doesn't work on me, big brother. She must be really under your skin for you to be this bent out of shape." When Brandon skewered him with another look, Khalil said, "Okay, okay. I can't wait for Vonnie and Morgan to find out." He shook his head. "The way you harassed them, they're gonna be all over you." He laughed again.

"I'm about two seconds from rearranging your pretty boy face." He started to comment further, but halted when Faith entered with his parents and uncle. She had on a navy blue dress that stopped at the knee and hugged every one of her luscious curves. His body reacted and he cursed under his breath. His gaze followed her as she took a seat on the other side of the table across from him. Her cold and angry eyes met his, and then she smoothly looked away.

Khalil whispered, "Guess she's not too happy with you either, Brandon, but she is stunning. I wouldn't mind sampling some of that beauty."

Brandon clenched his jaw so tight, pain radiated up the side of his face. One more word and he would snap. He scooted his chair over to put some distance between him and Khalil and closed his eyes briefly to maintain his composure. Why was he so upset? It was over between them, so he needed to move on. His father took his seat at the head of the table and started to speak.

"I can't tell you how happy I am today. We've been praying for this day to come for nearly three decades." Nolan nodded Thad's way.

Thad stood and helped Faith to her feet. "I'd like you all to meet my daughter, Faith Alexander. It's taken me twenty-eight years to find her again and it's been a long time coming." He gestured for Faith to speak and took his seat.

Faith looked around the room. "I am very glad to have my father in my life and overwhelmed by his generosity. I'll share a little about me. I grew up in Portland, Oregon, have a degree in business, completed a web design course and started my own company, Impressions Web Design, three years ago while working as an assistant manager in a small software company. Recently, I was able to quit my job and focus on my business full-time. I realize I don't know anything about home safety and some of you may be uncomfortable with an outsider coming in and assuming the role of vice president." She looked directly at Brandon. "So, I've decided not to take the job, but will honor part of my father's wish and succeed him on the advisory board." She sat.

Brandon should have been happy. She'd given him what he wanted, but somehow it felt hollow. Faith avoided looking at him for the remainder of the meeting and, when it was over, his family was quick to welcome her. Seeing her standing next to Uncle Thad, Brandon realized she looked a lot like him. Throughout the entire time, she never turned his way.

After Faith and Uncle Thad left, Justin came over to

Brandon. "Is there a coincidence that the woman you helped at the crash and this woman have the same name?"

"No."

"Well, at least she's not taking the job. Siobhan said you'd rather run the company alone. Although I can't understand how you'd mind seeing her at the office every day."

His father interrupted. "Faith is part of our family and will make a wonderful addition to the company with her background. And though she mentioned not taking the VP position, I'm hoping to convince her otherwise. Thank you for making her feel welcome. Your mother and I will be joining Thad and Faith for lunch. I'll be back this afternoon." His mom waved as they left, leaving Brandon, his siblings and in-laws alone.

Siobhan was in Brandon's face before the door closed good. "You were pretty rude to Faith. I know you think you should run the company alone, but you're going to have to get used to having her here."

"Unfortunately, Brandon's problems with Faith extend beyond the boardroom," Khalil said.

All eyes turned Brandon's way and Malcolm threw up his hands. "Good grief. What now?"

While they all looked on, Brandon told them how he met Faith, about their growing relationship and the blowout.

"And as usual, you jammed both feet in your mouth before a signal went to your brain," Morgan drawled. She shook her head. "I swear, Brandon, after all the trouble your mouth has gotten you in over the past three decades, you should have learned to think at least once before opening your big mouth."

Brandon didn't like having his shortcomings put on full blast, especially by his baby sister, who used to think he walked on water. He stood. "I'm going to my office."

Khalil followed suit. "Whatever. But you need to fix this. I'm going back to the gym."

He didn't know how to fix it, or if he even wanted to.

By Thursday, Brandon was as close to miserable as he had ever been. His concentration was shot and he hadn't gotten one thing done since arriving at six thirty that morning and it was eleven now. He got up and paced the confines of his office. Had he been unfair? He replayed the last conversation between him and Faith and kept seeing the hurt and anger in her eyes. He scrubbed a frustrated hand down his face. Brandon didn't know what he expected after he ended the relationship, but it wasn't her agreeing and showing him the door. Usually, there were tears, questions and, once, begging. But not Faith. He thought he could dismiss her just as easily as the others, but she had stolen his heart without even trying. He loved her and wanted her.

Brandon rounded the desk and dropped down in his chair. He couldn't eat, sleep, and his siblings were all mad at him. But what tore at him more than anything was hearing her give up her inheritance, what was rightfully hers because of him. He'd been selfish and felt lower than dirt. He had to talk to her. Picking up the phone, he started to dial, but hung up. This had to been done face-to-face. He rotated toward his computer and brought up his schedule for the afternoon. He had a meeting at two, which left him plenty of time to run by the hotel. He stopped by his dad's office to let him know he was leaving.

"Got a minute, Dad?"

His father looked up from the paper in his hand. "Sure."

Brandon came fully into the office and propped a hip on the desk. "I need to go out for a bit. I'll be back for the meeting with Marketing at two."

"That's fine. Oh, and don't think I didn't notice you at the meeting on Tuesday. I'm expecting you to do whatever it takes to make Faith feel welcome here. I'm not going to tell you how to do it, but I fully expect for you two to be straightened out by the retirement party."

His father gave Brandon a meaningful look and Brandon knew he was talking about more than the job. "I'm going to try, Dad. Thanks."

It took him forty minutes to get to the hotel and, by the time he knocked on the door, every fear and doubt he had rose to the surface. He lowered his head and gave himself a pep talk. His head jerked up when the door opened. She had on a pair of shorts and an oversized tee, and her hair had been pulled back in a loose ponytail, and the sight of her made his heart race.

Faith said nothing at first. Then, "What are you doing here?"

"May I come in? Please."

She backed up, and waved him in, and then stood with her arms folded. Waiting.

"I want to apologize for everything I said. I was wrong."

"Okay. Thanks for the apology. I need to finish packing."

His brow lifted. "Are you moving in with your dad?"

"No. I'm going home."

His fear magnified. He moved closer to her and reached for her hand. She took a step back. "I messed up, Faith. I don't want you to go, sweetheart. I love you. I was selfish and wrong. Dead wrong. That position belongs to you and you should take it."

She eyed him. "Why are you being so nice all of a sudden? Did your father put you up to this?"

Brandon let out a frustrated sigh. "No. I came because I love you and want you back."

"Brandon, I don't want your love because you feel guilty."

"That's not it. I'll admit to being guilty for shoving my feet in my mouth again, but my love for you is true."

Faith studied him a long moment, then shook her head. "I can't do this, Brandon. I think it's best we leave things the way they are. And you'll be happy that I'm not living here so you'll be free to run *your* company any way you want." Something like regret flickered in her eyes briefly, then it was gone. She cleared her throat. "If you'll excuse me, I need to finish packing. My plane leaves in the morning." She opened the door. "Goodbye, Brandon."

The tears in her eyes were killing him. Brandon wanted to take her in his arms and promise never to hurt her again. He lifted his hand to touch her and she shook her head. He dropped his hand, turned and walked out. She wouldn't even listen to him. On the drive back, he realized that must have been how she felt when he wouldn't listen.

Not quite ready for the workplace, Brandon stopped at a nearby park. He passed a children's area where a few toddlers were playing on the various climbing structures while their parents hovered nearby. He spotted a bench a few feet ahead and took a seat. A few minutes later, he realized he wasn't exactly dressed for sitting outdoors and rolled up the sleeves of his gray dress shirt and unbuttoned an additional button. The sun was at its zenith and, although the bench sat partially shaded by a large tree, beads of perspiration dotted his forehead.

Brandon let out a frustrated breath. For the first time in his life, he understood how it felt not to have someone listen. And it didn't feel good. Granted, he had stuck both feet into his mouth before a signal went to his brain, as Morgan had so eloquently pointed out. Now, he had lost the woman he loved. Faith was going home for good and there wasn't a damn thing he could do about it. He glanced down at his watch, sighed heavily and stood. He had no desire to sit in a meeting this afternoon, and the job he'd wanted for as long as he could remember suddenly didn't hold the same appeal.

Brandon retraced his steps to the car and drove to the office. He figured the time at the park would have improved his mood. But nothing had changed by the time he made it back and it was all he could do to get through the meeting. On the way back to his office, Siobhan intercepted him.

"We need to talk."

He didn't break stride. "I'm not in the mood to talk."

Siobhan followed him into his office and shut the door. "You don't need to be." Before he could reply, she said, "Sit down, Brandon, close your mouth and listen." They engaged in a staredown and Siobhan held his gaze unflinchingly until he reluctantly dropped down in the chair. "Tell me what happened between you and Faith."

Brandon really didn't want to talk about Faith, especially since he was still hurt by her rejection. "I helped her after she had the accident and was just being friendly. But then things changed." He told her about their dates, how much fun they had together, how he felt about her and how he'd messed up. He finished with, "And now she won't listen to me."

She smiled. "I guess Morgan was right. How does it feel being on this side of things? Have you apologized?"

"Yes, but she doesn't believe me or that I love her."

Her eyes widened and a smile lit her face. "Aww sookie sookie now! I thought I'd never see the day. Mom is going to be so excited."

Brandon groaned. "There's nothing to get excited about. Didn't you just hear what I said? She's going back home tomorrow. It's over."

Siobhan angled her head. "Do you really love her?"

"More than I ever thought possible."

"Okay. I'll get you another chance." She stood and pointed a finger his way. "So get yourself together, little brother."

He lifted a brow. "How?"

"Don't worry about it. Just make sure you don't blow it." And she sailed out.

He leaned back in his chair. If he got another chance, he was damn sure not going to blow it.

Chapter 19

Faith sat across from Kathi Sunday night at dinner pushing the food around her plate. She hadn't really wanted to go out, but Kathi insisted it would cheer her up. They'd even gone to the local bar and grill that served their favorite appetizer platter loaded with hot wings, loaded potato skins, fried zucchini and shrimp cocktail. However, none of it made her feel better. Faith turned as a loud cheer went up. A group of men sat at the bar watching a baseball game.

"How does it feel to be home?"

"Okay. My parents are glad to have me back and I've been working nonstop to catch up on my work."

"Have you talked to Brandon?"

"He's called twice since he came by the hotel Thursday. I think he's just feeling guilty because he didn't want me to take the job. I don't want to give him another chance to break my heart. It hurts too much," she added quietly.

Kathi placed her fork on the plate. "What if he's really sorry and seriously wants to get back together?"

"I just can't do it." She needed to get on with her life. She'd gotten an email from a retirement community wanting her to design their website and that would keep her busy and her mind off Brandon. They continued to eat in silence for a few minutes. "How's it going with Cameron?"

Kathi smiled. "It's going great. He's taking me to meet his family at their summer barbecue next weekend."

"That's great. Sounds like it's getting serious."

"I really like Cameron and I hope so."

They finished the meal and, with a promise to talk during the week, parted. On the way home, Faith thought about how happy Kathi sounded. She was elated for her friend, but it reminded Faith that she had another failed relationship to add to her growing list.

Her telephone was ringing when she unlocked the door to her home and she rushed to catch it.

"Hello."

"Hello, Faith? This is Siobhan Cartwright. How are you?"

"I'm fine. Thanks for asking." Had Brandon asked her to call? "What can I help you with?"

"Two things. One, I wanted to know if you had any questions about your new position and two, I wanted to make sure you were coming to the retirement party for our fathers. I know Uncle Thad will be happy to see you and it will give me and my sister and brothers more time to get to know you."

"I hadn't really planned to—"

"This will also be a good time for you to meet some of the other employees you'll be working with. You don't have to worry about your flight and hotel arrangements. I'll take care of them and email you the details. What's your email address?"

Faith rattled it off.

"If you have any questions, please feel free to give me

a call. I'll send you an email in the morning with all of my information. I look forward to seeing you again."

"Same here," Faith said, not believing that she had just agreed to go back to LA.

"Have a good evening, Faith."

"Thanks. You, too." She hung up, shook her head and remembered that this woman was the PR director and probably did this kind of thing in her sleep. And she was good at it. Faith wasn't looking forward to seeing Brandon, but reminded herself she was going for her father, not him. Now she needed to shop for a formal dress. Kathi was going to love that.

The phone rang again. She glanced down at the display and smiled upon seeing Thad's number. "Hey, Dad."

"Hey, baby. I wasn't sure if you knew about the retirement party and I wanted to make sure you're coming."

"I talked to Siobhan already and I'll be there."

"I'd like to invite your mother and father, as well."

Faith gasped in surprise. "I'll ask them." They talked a while longer about how she was dealing with the breakup and some of the things she would need to know about her position on the board, then ended the call.

She leaned back in the chair and tapped the phone against her chin. How would her parents react to the invitation? Her stepfather, ever the diplomat, would probably be okay, but she wasn't as sure about her mother. Even Faith felt a little uneasy about how things might play out. She loved all of her parents and the last thing she wanted or needed was more drama in her life. She'd have enough to deal with that night. And just thinking about it gave her a headache, so she turned her attention back to work.

Faith spent the remainder of the evening and the next day working on some preliminary logo designs for a client. She waited until late Monday afternoon to go visit her parents. Her mother worked as a school librarian and was off for the summer, and her dad worked at the post office.

Her mother greeted her with a strong hug and searched Faith's face. "How are you, sweetheart?"

"I'm okay, Mom." Faith turned to her father and greeted him the same way. "Hi, Daddy."

"Hey, baby. I'm glad to see you."

She took a seat on a chair opposite them. "I've been invited to attend the retirement party for my father and Nolan Gray two weeks from now." She looked at her mother. "Dad specifically invited you two."

Her mother frowned. "Us? Why?"

Faith shrugged. "He didn't say. Just that he really wanted you to come." She could see the wheels turning in her mother's head, trying to come up with an excuse to decline.

"I think that's a great idea, Francis," her father said. "Tell him we'll be there."

"Okay. I'll see about travel arrangements. Can you get off work, Dad?"

"I have enough leave time for three people. I'm sure they won't miss me for a couple of days."

She nodded. "I'll let you know when everything is set up."

He stood. "This grass isn't going to cut itself, so I'll leave you two to talk." He bent and kissed Faith's forehead, then placed a tender kiss on her mother's lips before going out back.

When they were alone, she turned to her mother. "Can I ask you a question?"

"Of course."

She didn't know a good way to ask, so she just blurted the question. "Mom, do you ever regret leaving?"

Her mom gave her a sympathetic smile. "If you're talking about Thad, then yes, for a long time. I loved Thad.

And like I told you, he was a *good* man, but I just didn't know how to deal with his illness." She studied Faith. "Why are you asking?"

Faith told her about the breakup with Brandon, how he had come to apologize and the fact that Faith didn't believe his apology was sincere.

Her mother left the sofa and, taking the chair next to Faith, grasped her hand. "If you love him and get a second chance, don't be a stubborn fool like me. Take it."

"Thanks, Mom." But she didn't think she had another chance after tossing him out her hotel room four days ago. For all she knew, he may have moved on and that meant she was too late. She shook off the negative thought. It couldn't be too late.

Brandon sat in his office late Monday afternoon beginning the task of boxing up his belongings to take to his new office and thinking about Faith. She still hadn't returned any of his calls.

Siobhan poked her head in the door. "Don't be here all night or I will come and escort you out." They shared a smile, recalling a time when he'd said the same thing to her.

"I won't. I'm just getting things ready for the transition. I plan to be out of here by seven."

"How's it going?"

"It's more than I thought, but I can handle it." They had promoted one of the managers to take over Brandon's current position and he had been working on detailed notes for when they met later in the week.

"Just so you know, Faith is coming to the retirement party. From what I understand, her parents will be here, too. So, it might be a good time to bring out all that irresistible charm you've always bragged about."

He chuckled. "The only problem with that approach is that she seems to be immune."

Siobhan laughed. "Well, there's only one thing left to do."

"What's that?"

She placed a hand on his heart. "Tell her what's in here. Oh, and remind her what she'd be missing without you. That's a little advice from Mom."

"Mom?"

"Yep. How do you think I got Justin back after I messed up? And this time, *listen* to Faith."

Brandon hugged her. "Thanks, sis."

"No problem. If you need some help, let me know." She tossed him a wink and left.

He smiled. There may be some hope for him after all.

Over the next two weeks, between daily meetings with his dad, training his replacement and packing, Brandon was so busy that he didn't have a chance to figure out a game plan to win Faith back. By the night of the party, he decided to take Siobhan's advice and just speak from his heart. It was all he had left.

Faith was nervous as she entered the hotel ballroom with her parents. There had to be at least five hundred people in attendance. She glanced around the elegant space with its high ceilings, stunning crystal chandeliers and walls appointed with gleaming dark wood and expensive fabric panels. There was even a dance floor in the center and a bar set up on the far side of the room.

"Do all these people work for the company?" her mother asked.

"I have no idea." She spotted Thad coming toward them, looking very handsome in his black tuxedo. She heard her mother gasp softly and smiled at her.

He held out his arms. "Faith, I'm so glad you came."

"Hi, Dad."

Thad turned to her mother. "Francis, it's been a long time. You're as beautiful as ever." He kissed her cheek.

"Thank you. It's good to see you, Thad."

Faith introduced her stepfather.

The two men shook hands and Thad said, "William and Francis, you did an outstanding job raising Faith. She's amazing."

Faith's mother visibly relaxed and she reached out and hugged him. "Thank you, Thad. And thank you for the invitation. Congratulations on your retirement."

"Yes, thank you and congratulations," William echoed.

Thad took them over to meet Nolan and DeAnna Gray and Faith went to get something to drink.

"Hi, Faith. Glad you could make it," a voice said behind her.

She spun around. "Hi, Morgan."

"This is my husband, Omar Drummond."

"Nice to meet you, Faith," he said.

"Same here, Omar." The football player was gorgeous with his towering height, bronze skin and flowing locks.

One by one, all the Gray siblings drifted over to say hello. She also had a chance to meet Siobhan's handsome husband, Justin, the inventor. She saw everyone except Brandon, but didn't want to ask about him. They all stood there talking while sipping champagne.

A few minutes later, Faith spotted Brandon across the room and choked on the drink. In his formal wear, with his sexy good looks, he was hard to miss. More than a few women stopped him and one particular woman sidled up to him and pressed her body close, making Faith see red. She was tempted to march over and snatch that weave out the woman's head. She drained the drink, set the glass on the table with a thud and went to find a bathroom, muttering under her breath. Why did seeing another woman with

Brandon make her so angry if she claimed to be moving on with her life? Faith had lied to herself. She didn't want to move on, not without Brandon. She loved him. As her emotions bubbled up, she closed her eyes. Composing herself, she went back to the ballroom. Everyone was headed to his or her table for dinner. She went to go sit with her parents, but Siobhan stopped her, directed her to the head table and seated her next to Brandon.

"I think you two have already met." Siobhan smiled and strolled off.

Just sitting next to him conjured up everything she felt for this man.

Brandon turned her way and scanned her from head to toe. "How've you been?"

"Okay."

"That makes one of us. I can't sleep. I miss hearing your voice, seeing your smile. I just miss you, Faith."

"I don't know what to say. I…" The servers placed their plates in front of them before she could comment further. Faith thanked the server. They had spared no expense—beef tenderloin, chicken breast with a lemon caper sauce, herb roasted fingerling potatoes and steamed green beans.

Khalil Gray took the chair on the other side of her. "Well hello, Faith. You look absolutely gorgeous. I think I got the best seat in the house."

Over the course of dinner, Faith found out that Khalil designed accessible equipment for his gym, had a great sense of humor and flirted as easily as he breathed.

"If you're going to be in town for a while, maybe we can get together for dinner," Khalil continued.

She shook her head. "I'm only here for the party tonight."

Brandon leaned forward and directed a glare at his brother. Khalil just smiled and kept right on playing.

If that look was any indication, Faith sensed that Brandon wasn't too thrilled with his brother's antics. She just concentrated on her food.

At the conclusion of dinner, each sibling gave tributes to their father.

Mr. Gray spoke next, thanking all of the employees, children and his wife. He laughingly told her, "Anna, now we have plenty of time for that Caribbean cruise we've been putting off."

She responded with a resounding, "Hallelujah!" eliciting laugher throughout the room.

Her father was next and echoed Mr. Gray's sentiments. "I'm proud to be called Uncle, but tonight is very special because my daughter is here. Stand up, Faith."

Heat stung Faith's face. She wasn't expecting to be singled out, but stood, did a quick wave and sat.

"She will be representing me on the board and I believe she will be a great asset to the company." Thad concluded his speech and reclaimed his seat.

Mr. Gray rose again to pass the mantel. "It gives me great pleasure to pass the torch to my son Brandon Gray." He directed his comments to Brandon. "Son, be a servant leader. Your job is to make those around you better." Mr. Gray faced the audience. "I'm confident he will lead this company well and continue the great work we started. Brandon?"

Brandon stood and joined his father at the podium to thunderous applause. He shook his father's hand and hugged him. "Thank you, Dad. I'm humbled by your faith in me and will try not to let you down. Most of you who know me know I like to work alone, but my dad reminded me that no one can do it alone." He shifted his gaze to Faith. "You need great people by your side, ones who will make you better."

Khalil whispered to Faith, "Guess this means we won't get that date, beautiful."

She shifted her confused gaze to Khalil. "What?"

He smiled knowingly. "Big brother just threw down the gauntlet."

Turning back, Faith barely heard the rest of Brandon's speech, wondering what he meant by needing *great people by your side, ones who will make you better.*

Shortly after Brandon finished his speech, the music started and people took to the dance floor. Many of the company employees came up to the table to welcome her. There were so many that, after a while, the names and faces started to blur.

Khalil his extended his hand. "Would you like to dance?"

She hesitated briefly, then placed her hand in his. "Um, sure."

Out on the floor, they moved to the slow tune. When the song ended, he said, "Thanks for the dance. This may have been my only chance to dance with you…until the wedding, that is." He chuckled, winked and took her back to the table.

Before she could ask him what he meant, he disappeared in the crowd. Faith danced with her stepfather next, then Brandon's youngest brother, Malcolm, and finally, her father.

"I think Brandon is beginning to realize what's important," Thad said. "I told you that love would always find a way."

"Is that right?" Yes, he'd mentioned needing great people while looking at her, but she hadn't wanted to read anything into it. But had he been talking about something other than work? Did she dare hope?

"Yes. And I think you will do well together." He escorted her over to where Brandon stood on the dance floor.

"Thanks, Unc. I'll take good care of her."

"I expect no less, son."

Faith stood there trying to figure out what was going on. Brandon slid his arm around her waist and started a slow sway. A flood of memories engulfed her—what she'd missed, how his touch made her feel. She missed the warmth of his hands gently caressing her spine, his hard body pressed against hers, the steady beat of his heart. The last time he'd held her this way had ended with him making love to her all night.

As if hearing her thoughts, Brandon said, "I missed holding you in my arms, feeling your heart against mine." He held her close and continued moving.

She laid her head on his shoulder and melted into him, savoring being held this way. She wished it could be like this always.

"Come take a walk with me," he said when the song ended. He took her hand and led her out of the ballroom and to the hotel's garden area. They walked along the path a short distance, and then he stopped and pulled her in front of him. "I practiced all day what I wanted to say to you and now…now the only thing I can think about is how much I've missed you." He tilted her chin and locked his eyes with hers. "How much I love you and need you in my life."

"Brandon," Faith whispered.

"I should have listened to you, shouldn't have forced you to give up what rightly belongs to you. If I had to do it all again, I'd give it all up just to have you." He paused as if trying to bring his emotions under control. "Faith, I thought having that job was the most important thing in my life, but you mean more to me than anything. And I don't care about running the company, if it means I can't have you."

Faith was speechless. His passionate confession went straight to her heart. "Are you saying…?"

"Yes. I'm saying I love you and whether you take the

job or not, it will always be there for you and so will I. Please give me another chance to show you how much you mean to me."

"I…yes. I love you, Brandon." She heard his soft gasp of relief just before he lowered his head and kissed her with a searing intensity that left them both trembling.

Brandon brushed tender kisses along her face. "Thank you for giving me another chance, baby. How long are you going to be here?"

"Until Sunday," she murmured against his lips. "Why?"

"Can we spend some time together tomorrow?" His lips continued to roam lazily over her neck and shoulder.

As she ran her hands over his broad chest, she wanted nothing more than to spend the rest of tonight reacquainting herself with every part of his body, but she'd settle for the next day. "I'd like that."

He eased back. "I'll pick you up around eleven. Is that okay?"

It was better than okay. She had the man she loved back in her life.

"What are we doing here?" Faith asked the next morning as Brandon parked in the underground garage of the company's office building.

Brandon got out, came around and helped her out of the car. "You'll see."

She narrowed her eyes. "You're smiling. What are you up to?"

He gave her a quick kiss and pressed the elevator button. "I'm smiling because I have you back in my life."

"Mmm-hmm." They rode the elevator up and exited on the same floor as she had on her first visit. With it being a Saturday, they were the only people there. She followed him down the long hallway to a set of double doors.

He opened the doors with a flourish and gestured her inside. "What do you think?"

The spacious office had a large, polished mahogany desk, a window that extended the length of one wall, a bookshelf and another equally polished table on the other side of the room with seating for four. "It's fabulous. Is this your new office?"

"Yes. But this isn't what I really wanted to show you." He walked over to an inner door and opened it. "Come with me."

Faith tentatively followed him through the door, which accessed another office that was no less opulent but had been done in lighter colors. "Whose office is this?"

"Yours."

She spun around. *"Mine?"*

Brandon went behind the desk and pulled out the leather chair. "Have a seat."

She sat and ran her hand lightly along the edge of the desk. It was beautiful and the chair fit perfectly.

"I know you're still growing your business, so I thought the office could serve a dual purpose."

She stared at him. He was really making it hard for her not to take the job, though she had been talking to her father more about it and had become intrigued with the possibilities. "So, what would my role in the company be?"

He regarded her silently for a moment. "To act in my stead when I'm not here, help me take our company into the future and continue to make it one of the best anywhere."

"And you'd trust me to do all of that?"

"Yes," he answered without hesitation.

She smiled.

"There's something else. Look in the drawer."

Faith scooted back and pulled the center compartment open. Her heart skipped a beat and her gaze flew to his. She brought her hands to her mouth and stared at the small jeweler's box surrounded by rose petals the same color as those he had that beautiful night at his house.

When she didn't make a move, Brandon chuckled, reached around her and removed the ring. He lowered himself to one knee next to her. "I love you, Faith, and I need you. Marry me, baby. I promise to give you my all from this moment forward."

Tears misted her eyes and she cupped his face. "I love you and need you, too, Brandon. Yes, I'll marry you." He lifted her hand and slid the sparkling solitaire surrounded by smaller diamonds onto her finger. "It's *amazing*." She threw her arms around him and kissed him with all her heart.

"Thank you for making this so easy because I wasn't taking no for an answer."

Faith laughed. "I see Mr. Bossy is back."

"Yeah, but I'm sure you'll have no problems keeping me in line."

"No. No, I won't."

Brandon wiggled his eyebrows. "How about we christen our new offices?"

She gasped. "We can't do *that* in *here*."

"Why not? There's no one here but us." He disappeared through the connecting door, came back in a flash, locked the other door and placed her on the empty desk. He undid the buttons on her top, undid her bra and took one taut nipple into the warmth of his mouth. "Now, what were you saying?"

The only thing she managed was a strangled moan as their clothes disappeared and he entered her with one powerful thrust. "I love you, Brandon."

"I love you, too, Faith. You are my heart."

Epilogue

Six months later

Brandon stood at the end of the aisle in the filled church sanctuary anxiously waiting for Faith to appear. Between Faith relocating to LA and both of them getting acclimated to their new positions, he'd had to wait six long months to make her his wife. And every one of those days tested his patience in ways he couldn't begin to describe.

The door opened and his breath caught. He didn't think Faith could be more beautiful, but today she looked absolutely radiant. The white strapless dress she wore flowed to the floor, emphasized her full breasts, small waist and flaring hips. Brandon didn't realize he had taken a step until he felt the tug on his arm.

"Easy, big brother," Khalil whispered. "You're supposed to wait for her to come to you."

He glanced over his shoulder and met his brother's smile, then turned back to watch his bride. She hadn't wanted the traditional wedding march played and, instead, had chosen "Setembro (Brazilian Wedding Song)" by Quincy Jones. The rhythm fit perfectly with the subtle sway of her hips as she glided toward him on the arms of both her fathers. She smiled at him and his heart nearly beat out of his chest.

When she finally made it to him, it took all of Brandon's restraint not to take her into his arms and kiss her the way he'd described on their erotic phone call last night. Since their mothers wouldn't let them see each other after the rehearsal and dinner, it was the best they could do.

As if reading his mind, Faith shook her head and mouthed, "Don't you do it."

She knew him all too well. But she also knew he called his own shots. Before he could stop himself, he seized her mouth in a searing kiss. He poured everything he felt for her in it, wanting her to know that from now on this was how it would be between them. The minister cleared his throat, but Brandon didn't immediately stop. Finally, he lifted his head and told the man, "I'm ready now."

The minister shook his head. "More than ready, in my estimation."

Khalil and Malcolm chuckled.

The ceremony took less than twenty minutes and Brandon stared into the eyes his new wife. "I love you, Mrs. Gray." Their first kiss as husband and wife was filled with love and anticipation of what was to come.

Faith smiled up at him. "I love you, too. But I don't know what I'm going to do with you."

He swept her into his arms and strode up the aisle. "Well, you'll have a lifetime to figure it out."

She threw her head back and laughed.

Brandon caught Justin's gaze as he sat holding his newborn daughter. His brother-in-law's words rushed back to Brandon: *Whatever you do, don't let her get away.*

Justin smiled and nodded.

Brandon now understood what Justin had meant. When he thought he'd lost Faith, nothing else seemed to matter. Holding her in his arms now, he knew that he'd found the woman who was meant for him, the one he'd give everything to and the one he would love for the rest of his life.

* * * * *

She's got sky-high ambitions to match the glamorous penthouses she shows, but real estate agent Angela Trainor keeps both feet firmly on the ground. Her attraction to her sexy boss, Daniel Cobb, needs to remain at bay or it could derail her promising career. But when Daniel takes Angela under his wing, their mutual admiration could become a sizzling physical connection...

Read on for a sneak peek at
MIAMI AFTER HOURS,
the first exciting installment of
Harlequin Kimani Romance's continuity
MILLIONAIRE MOGULS OF MIAMI!

"Now you just have to seal the deal and get to closing." He knew that just because an offer had been made didn't mean the sale was a foregone conclusion. Deals could fall apart at any time. Not that it ever happened to him. Daniel took every precaution to ensure that it didn't.

"Of course."

"Speaking of deals, I've recently signed a new client, a developer that has tasked me with selling out the eighty condos in his building in downtown Miami."

Angela's eyes grew large. "Sounds amazing."

"It is, but it's a challenge. The lower-end condos go for a thousand a square foot, and the penthouse is fifteen hundred a square foot."

"Well, if anyone can do it, you can."

Daniel appreciated her ego boost. "Thank you, but praise is not the reason I'm mentioning it."

"No?" She quirked a brow and he couldn't resist returning it with a grin.

"I want you to work on the project with me."

"You do?" Astonishment was evident in her voice.

"Why do you think I plucked you away from that other firm? It was to give you the opportunity to grow and to learn under my tutelage."

"I'm ready for whatever you want to offer me." She blushed as soon as she said the words, no doubt because he could certainly take it to mean something other than work. Something like what he could offer her in the bedroom.

Where had that thought come from?

It was his cardinal rule to never date any woman in the workplace. Angela would be no different. He didn't mix business with pleasure.

He banished the thought and finally replied, "I'm sure you are." Then he walked over to his desk, procured a folder and handed it to her. "Read this. It'll fill you in on the development. Let's plan on putting our heads together on a marketing strategy tomorrow after you've had time to digest it."

Angela nodded and walked toward the door. "And, Daniel?"

"Yes?"

"Thank you for the opportunity."

Don't miss MIAMI AFTER HOURS
by Yahrah St. John, available June 2017
wherever Harlequin® Kimani Romance™
books and ebooks are sold.

Get 2 Free Books,
Plus 2 Free Gifts—
just for trying the
Reader Service!

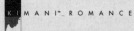